FOUND IN THE ATTIC

Dorothy Emily Stevenson, born in Edinburgh in 1892, was very proud of her family tradition of engineering and writing; her great-grandfather, Robert Stevenson, designed the famous Bell Rock Lighthouse and many others around the Scottish coast, and her father was a first cousin of Robert Louis Stevenson. She herself started writing stories as a small child,

Her first novel, *Peter West,* was published in 1929, but she did not find fame until 1932 with the publication of *Mrs. Tim of the Regiment* based on her own experience as an army wife with her husband Captain James Peploe, whom she had married in 1916. She went on to write a total of 45 (published) novels, which sold over seven million copies and brought her worldwide fame.

The extent of her early writing is becoming more evident with the recent discovery of some boxes of unpublished manuscripts, including *The Fair Miss Fortune, Emily Dennistoun* and *Portrait of Saskia* in her grand-daughter's attic.

The family moved to Moffat in the Scottish Borders in 1940, where she wrote her books in longhand, reclining on a sofa looking out over the Dumfriesshire hills.

She died in 1973.

FOUND
IN THE ATTIC

D. E. STEVENSON

Greyladies

Published by
Greyladies
an imprint of The Old Children's Bookshelf
175 Canongate, Edinburgh EH8 8BN

First published 2013
© The Estate of D. E. Stevenson
Design and layout © Shirley Neilson 2013
Foreword © Jerri Chase 2013

ISBN   978-1-907503-28-3

Set in Sylfaen / Perpetua
Printed and bound CPI Group (UK) Ltd, Croydon, CRO 4YY

CONTENTS

"Found in the Attic"

2013 marks the 40th anniversary of the death of D. E. Stevenson in 1973. Most authors of what some critics call "middle brow women's novels" have been forgotten by the time they have stopped writing for 20 years, much less 40. Yet, here we are celebrating the fifth "new" book by Stevenson to be published since 2011, from material "found in the attic" and not published during her lifetime.

There exists a substantial fan base for D. E. Stevenson and her works. Some of these devoted readers are members of an email list which discusses her life and books. This group refers to themselves as "the DESsies". In addition to online activities, a large number of physical gatherings have taken place, ranging from two people meeting for tea and book talk to 20 or more DESsies from several countries getting together, for example in Boston in 2007 and Edinburgh in 2010. Every one of these meetings have been enjoyed by the participants, and those times we have been able to also meet with descendants of D. E. Stevenson or visit the house where she lived or locations used in her books have been very special. This group, as well as countless other fans, were delighted at the publication of the "found in the attic" books, letting us do something we had never imagined doing, read NEW to us writings by this special author.

Why do we care about what was "found in the attic"? What is it about the novels of D. E. Stevenson that inspire those who love her work to be so dedicated? And why are these works worth publishing, perhaps 80 or more years after they were written?

There are many reasons; each reader has their own. I will give you some of mine.

Stevenson's novels seem to be simple stories, often about seemingly ordinary people. However, this simplicity is deceptive. It took a great deal of skill to write something so easy to read and so straightforward as to appear naïve, yet able to create a believable world inhabited by believable characters, able to stand the test of repeated re-reading.

Stevenson's books always have evocative descriptions of locations including both countryside and houses. Many of her books are set, all or in part, in what is clearly the Scottish Borders. Many of her towns and villages are inspired at least in part by Moffat, where she lived for many years. Other settings include London, the Scottish Highlands, Edinburgh, and France. As I read the descriptive portions of the novels I feel like I am traveling on holiday, to somewhere delightful. My real travels in England and Scotland, including several trips to Moffat, have shown me just how accurately her descriptions convey this sense of place.

A specific example is *The Young Mrs. Savage,* with the major location given as "Seatown". When I visited North Berwick, I would have recognized the town even if I hadn't known that the entire Stevenson family spent holidays there for many years. After just a few minutes in nearby Tantallon Castle I understood how, when the two young Savage children went there, they could forget about lunch and the need to get home until *much* too late to catch the bus.

An overwhelming reason DESsies read and re-read Stevenson's novels is her characters. They are very real to us, indicating that she must have been a very keen observer of the human condition. The characters and their backgrounds, motivations and possible futures are often under discussion on the DESsie email list. We feel that the characters are friends; we really care about them.

The ways in which her characters deal with the rigors of WWII is a recurring theme in Stevenson's novels. DESsies are particularly taken by the books written early in WWII, when the outcome of the war was uncertain. The writing of books such as *Mrs. Tim Carries On*, *Spring Magic* and *The English Air,* when faced with the possibility of invasion, is a remarkable achievement. Yet, Stevenson seldom allowed the horrors of war to overcome her kindness or that of her characters. In *Spring Magic*, fishermen go out in small boats to attempt to rescue the crew of a German plane that had fallen into the sea, and at the end of *Listening Valley*, Tonia was worried about not only the young pilot she was soon to marry, but also for all those on both sides who were facing loss: "It was the sorrow of the whole world that moved Tonia's heart tonight, it seemed to her that the world was tired and sick, that the whole of creation was suffering."

I believe that there is a segment of the reading public that isn't being well served by the majority of modern "main stream" adult fiction, with its focus on explicit sex, violence and the darker and more twisted aspects of life.

Stevenson's books can be enjoyed by readers who want books with clear moral and ethical standards, but without preaching. As D. M. McFarlan put it, when writing about Stevenson in *Delicious Prose* (a book mainly about the works of Angela Thirkell) Stevenson's books are filled with "the excellent standards of the Scottish gentlewoman". These standards provide the books with an overall moral and ethical background. Honesty, courage and kindness, especially in difficult times, seem to be among the primary of these standards. The standards can relate to choosing one's spouse/life partner, showing that shared values and mutual respect are needed, in addition to love. Stevenson's books provide happy endings without being overly sentimental or cloying.

Added to all of this is Stevenson's sense of humor. While *Miss Buncle's Book* and *Miss Buncle Married* are probably the most obviously and overtly funny of her novels, Stevenson used humor to leaven all of her work. As she said in the preface to *The Four Graces* (the fourth book in the Miss Buncle series), when asked "Is this a funny book?", "life is a funny business altogether (both funny-peculiar and funny-ha-ha)". Even the most serious of Stevenson's novels have passages that make the reader laugh, or at least give a contented smile. Much of this humor is character driven. That is, it isn't so much what is said or done, but it is *these* people saying or doing *this*.

Another indication of the staying power of D. E. Stevenson's works is their spread to types of media not imagined in her lifetime. Some of her works have long been put into braille and/or the special talking books for the blind. With the advent of personal computers and advanced software, those with special needs have been able to scan books and have a computerized voice read it to them. Now, anyone who owns a Nook, Kindle or other eReader can get several titles in eBook format, with more apparently on the way.

In the past, only a few D. E. Stevenson novels were available as cassette audiobooks, read by skilled professionals. Now, at last count sixteen of her novels are available as digital audiobooks, that can be downloaded to devices such as a smart phone, mp3 player, etc.

I previously mentioned the email group, which one can join by going to YahooGroups.com, or by sending an email to: DEStevenson-subscribe@yahoogroups.com. There are several websites devoted to D. E. Stevenson and her works. One of these, www.destevenson.org, maintained by DESsie Susan Daly, contains links to several others. In addition, there are at least two Stevenson inspired Facebook pages: https://www.facebook.com/groups/18730565731/) and an article in Wikipedia.

The internet even allows the fan to see D. E. Stevenson act in a film! The Scottish Screen Archive allows one to view the 1930 film *Fickle Fortune*, for which Stevenson wrote the "scenario", and in which she, using her married name Dorothy Peploe, acted a part. Her daughter Rosemary also acted in this film.
See: http://ssa.nls.uk/film.cfm?fid=0509.

D. E. Stevenson is certainly part of the 21st Century!

Found in the Attic is a bit different from the other Greyladies books of newly discovered D. E. Stevenson writings published to date. I have not yet had the chance to read all of the material included, but from the parts I have sampled, it seems that this collection of short stories, poems, plays and essays will provide a very interesting glimpse into the mind and personality of D. E. Stevenson. The biographical sketch and essays about her views on writing and about some of her specific books provide an obvious sort of insight, as she is describing herself and her work for an audience.

Some of the short stories and humorous plays and poems give a more personal view. In "Marriage Bells or Murder", apparently written after she had suffered some unfortunate reviews, Stevenson strands an author and a book critic on a desert island, and shows her feelings about each! The short plays, possibly written for a drama or film club (like she was part of in the making of *Fickle Fortune*) or to be performed as family entertainment, not only make the reader laugh, but demonstrate her ability to make light hearted use of a concept that she could use in a more serious way in her novels. I would guess that the very funny poem "Mister McGibbon's Daughter" may well have been written to entertain her family with a live performance.

Finally, the family photos included as illustrations to the book, also help bring the reader closer to D. E. Stevenson and her family. I will prize this book, as it provides a window into the life and times of my favorite author.

Jerri Chase, March 2013

FOUND IN THE ATTIC

MARRIAGE BELLS
– OR MURDER

MARRIAGE BELLS – OR MURDER

AN AUTHOR AND A CRITIC had the misfortune to be wrecked upon a desert island. The typhoon, which was the cause of the disaster, swept them onto the beach and left them high and dry. It then departed to continue its work of destruction elsewhere. The author was the first to regain his senses; he opened his eyes and discovered, somewhat to his surprise, that he was still alive. The sun was beating down upon him, and his clothes, though somewhat tattered, were almost dry. He sat up and looked round: before him was a lagoon, incredibly blue and calm, protected from the Pacific breakers by a coral reef; behind him were palm trees, tall and slim, their bright green foliage patterned boldly against the azure sky.

The author at once realised the situation; he knew all about desert islands, for he had written a story about one in his extreme youth. He was aware that the first thing to do was to explore the island. He did so, and found the usual amenities: a sufficient supply of coconut palms laden with fruit, complete with monkeys to deliver them when required; edible parrots, so tame that they could easily be knocked down with a stone; a spring of fresh water that bubbled out from between two rocks; a large bread-fruit tree and a small plantation of bananas. He also found a hut containing the skeleton of a man.

The author knew that all the best desert islands were provided with huts and skeletons, so he was neither

3

surprised nor distressed at the discovery. He went into the hut and found a table and a chair and a cupboard, all rudely fashioned from the native wood. He knew, of course, what the cupboard would contain, namely needles and thread, fishing hooks and lines, knives and cooking pots, paper and ink, and perhaps a lamp — in fact everything that was necessary to support life in reasonable comfort. He looked into the cupboard to make sure that everything was there, and was not disappointed.

By this time the critic had also recovered from his experiences. He found himself somewhat bruised, but otherwise unhurt. The sun was extremely hot, so he moved into the shade of a coconut palm and sat down. When the author returned to the beach he found the critic sitting there regarding the blue lagoon with a jaundiced eye.

The author was quite glad to find that the cast consisted of two players. He had looked all over the island but had found no trace of human occupation—except of course the skeleton which could not be called companionable. There was not even a footprint to be found. Being of a philosophical mind he had reconciled himself to the inevitable and decided that the play was to be of the Robinson Crusoe type, i.e., solitary exile. He would have to catch a parrot—or perhaps a monkey—and tame it. The prospect was slightly dull, the more so because the author was a sociable kind of man; he liked an audience—so many authors do—even Robinson Crusoe had an audience in the faithful Friday.

The author was, therefore, quite glad to see the critic

sitting up and taking notice. It meant rearranging his ideas, of course, but he was used to rearranging his ideas to meet the requirements of editors and publishers, so that it was no trouble to him at all. He would have preferred almost any type of man rather than a critic to share his solitude—a butcher, a baker, a carpenter, or a doctor would have been more use to him in his present circumstances, and almost any other type of man would have made a better audience, but beggars cannot be choosers, and a typhoon is no respecter of persons. The author decided to make the best of it, and, since it was important to start well, he greeted the critic in a friendly manner and asked how he was feeling.

The critic did not reply; he was still gazing malevolently at the blue lagoon. "I suppose it's real," he said at last. "It isn't a nightmare by any chance."

"A nightmare!" exclaimed the author in surprise. "Why should you think it was a nightmare? We're lucky to be alive after such a storm. Here we are, comfortably settled upon a desert island with all the usual—"

He was interrupted by a groan from his companion.

"Don't tell me there's a spring of fresh water."

"Yes, of course there is, a beautiful, clear crystal—"

"And coconuts? . . . and a bread fruit tree? Oh my God!"

The author was quite at sea as to why the critic should take exception to the island. Could the excitement of the shipwreck, and the shock of the sudden immersion have turned his brain?

"Perhaps you will feel better presently," he suggested

sympathetically.

"I shall probably feel worse," declared the critic.

"No, no—you will feel better. You need some food—"

"Be quiet!" cried the critic. "You don't understand—you don't even begin to understand the horror of the situation. I've read thousands of desert island stories—thousands and thousands—"

"But everybody likes them," objected the author in amazement. "Why, I wrote one myself—"

"I know, I know."

"And it was a best-seller—"

"I know."

"Well then!"

"I'm sick of them," declared the critic. "They are banal, they are overdone, they are hackneyed to the point of nausea."

"There's a hut with a skeleton in it," continued the author, trying to interest his companion in the discoveries he had made. "A hut with a skeleton—I shouldn't wonder if there was buried treasure—"

Silence fell—there was no more to say. They could hear the palm trees rustling in the evening breeze and the hollow boom of the Pacific rollers breaking upon the coral reef.

Several days passed. The author settled down quite happily; he bathed and fished in the calm waters of the lagoon; he amused himself by fashioning bowls out of coconut shells; he caught a parrot and spent hours trying to teach it to speak. He had managed to light a fire with a burning glass which he had found in the skeleton's hut; he provided the food and cooked it. The critic was still gloomy, still depressed by the hackneyed situation. He took no part in the preparation of the meals, nor in any of the author's domestic arrangements. He would not even explore the island, declaring that he knew already exactly what it was like. The weather continued perfect—calm, sunny, warm—not a cloud marred the cerulean blue of the sky.

On the evening of the fourth day the two men were eating their supper by the fire. It burnt brightly in the little clearing in front of the hut. (The skeleton had been removed from the hut and decently buried).

"I wonder how long we shall be here," remarked the author as he handed the critic his share of the meal—a fish, cooked to a turn and tastefully arranged on a plantain leaf. "I wonder how long we shall be here, and what the end of it will be."

"There are only three endings, and they have all been used a hundred times," replied the critic. "I really cannot get up the least enthusiasm about it."

"This might end differently."

"Impossible. Quite impossible. There is nothing new under the sun. Either a ship comes and takes us off, or else it doesn't come and we remain here until we die, or go mad, or until one of us goes mad and kills the other."

"Supposing savages—" began the author.

"That has been done too. Savages in war canoes. They beach their canoes on the strand and carouse all night, feasting and dancing."

"You mean cannibals?" enquired the author with an

involuntary shudder.

"My dear fellow, of *course*. Who ever read a South Sea Island story in which the savages were not cannibals? I believe that in real life very few of these tribes are devourers of human flesh, but we are not dealing with real life."

"We ought to have a look for the buried treasure," said the author, frowning thoughtfully.

"Do so by all means," answered the critic. "It is quite immaterial to me how you occupy your time."

The author did not reply. For one thing he thought the last remark distinctly ungrateful. The critic did not care how he occupied his time, but seemed quite pleased to accept the fruits of his labours, namely the excellent meals which were provided at regular intervals. For another thing the author's mouth was full of fish—it was excellent fare and he was extremely hungry. The life suited him, he had never felt so well. He could not help thinking that if the critic would get to work and find something to do he would feel less liverish and gloomy.

A few more days passed, and the author began to feel the urge to write. There was no reason why he should resist such a natural impulse. He found writing materials in the skeleton's hut and proceeded to indite a full account of all that had happened. The exercise of his talent gave him pleasure. He enjoyed describing the island, he took great pains in phrasing his story, writing and rewriting every sentence until he was completely satisfied with it. There was no hurry about it, of course, no hurry at all.

It was unfortunately impossible to finish the story, for he did not know how it would end—the end was on the knees of the Gods so to speak. This irked the author, it worried him considerably for he was in the habit of working out his stories in a methodical manner, embodying the end in the beginning and leading up to the climax—he was, in fact, extremely old fashioned in his art.

One day the author, having caught the fish for dinner and laid the foundations of the meal, returned to the hut to put in a couple of hours work upon his manuscript. He was surprised to find the critic, sitting in the skeleton's chair turning over the leaves of his story.

"You've no business to read that!" he cried, advancing into the hut in a belligerent manner.

"No business!" exclaimed the critic in amazement. "But it *is* my business. You don't seem to realise how fortunate you are to have a critic to read your stuff. Here you are, cast away upon a desert island with the one man who is absolutely necessary to your art."

The author had never considered that critics were absolutely necessary to his art, in fact he had always been of the opinion that they were rather a nuisance—an unavoidable nuisance of course, but definitely troublesome. On the other hand he saw that the critic had only spoken the truth in saying that it was his business to read the books of authors, and he saw that he had no grounds for complaint—he was a reasonable man.

"Well, what do you think of it?" he enquired.

"I shall write a review of it, of course."

"But what do you think of it?"

"Banal, and precious," declared the critic. "The characterisation is weak—you haven't got me at all—the book is not worth my while really. I should give it to one of my staff to do. Unfortunately I have no staff at present, so I shall be obliged to review the thing myself."

"Pray do not trouble—" began the author, trembling with rage at the insult to his book.

"I hope I know my duty," declared the critic. He rose briskly and departed with the manuscript under his arm.

It did not take the critic long to compose a short review of the story. He handed it to the author after supper. It was the kind of review that the author particularly disliked; the tone was superior, the style was flippant. The author read it and was justifiably annoyed.

"Look here," he began. "The story isn't finished yet—"

"Isn't it?" enquired the critic in surprise.

"Surely you saw that when you read it?"

"I never noticed—" the critic said witheringly. "In any case I should not have read more than six chapters of a tale like that. Six chapters were quite enough—" He shuddered elaborately, and then added, "But why didn't you finish it?"

"Because I didn't know how to end it."

"My dear fellow it is obvious to the meanest intelligence."

"How does it end, then?" demanded the author, too interested in the ending of the story to heed the insults which had been heaped upon himself and his work.

The critic smiled in a sphinx-like manner and shrugged

his shoulders. "That's your business, surely," he replied.

The author saw that this was true; it *was* his business to finish the story. He seized the manuscript and departed to the woods. For some time he walked about, scarcely seeing where he was going. I can make the story end as I like, he thought, but how? The story had gripped him now, his imagination wrestled with the problem. He was uplifted by the thought that he had the power to finish it as he pleased. An author was a god—almost. He could take life and mould it as he wanted; the critic was a poor worm compared with him, and, as a worm, beneath contempt.

At last he found the inspiration which he sought. He ran to the skeleton's hut, lighted the lamp, seized the pen and began to write.

The author wrote all night; the tropical dawn found him haggard and weary but still writing. He finished the story, laid down the pen, went out into the woods and flung himself down upon the ground. In a few moments he was sound asleep.

The critic woke at the usual hour and was extremely annoyed to find that his breakfast was not ready. He waited about, hoping that the author would appear, but at last the pangs of hunger overcame his pride and he strolled up to the hut to find out what had happened. The hut was empty, but the finished manuscript lay upon the table, an eloquent testimony of the manner in which the author had misspent the night.

So that's what it is! said the critic to himself. He

scanned the closely written leaves and decided that the end of the story was worse than all the rest put together—it was sentimental tripe. The author had finished the story as he wanted it to finish and this was how he had done it. He had evoked a beautiful young girl, a sort of Rima, wild and shy as a fawn. This lovely creature was in reality the daughter of the skeleton, whose hut was proving so useful to the shipwrecked *litterateurs*. When her father died the girl was only a child, she had run away from the terrifying Spectre of Death and had made her home with the monkeys in the impenetrable jungle at the farther end of the island. Years had passed, and the child grew to maidenhood. She was quite illiterate, of course, scarcely vocal. She was a blank page, she was a child of nature unsophisticated as a flower. This beautiful savage perceived the author from between the leaves of the banana trees. She was irresistibly attracted. She came out from her hiding place and prattled to him in the delightful baby language which was all that she could remember-of human speech. Of course she fell in love with him at once—what more natural? And she did not conceal her passion—concealment was unknown to her primitive nature. Here was a man—the first man she had seen—here was her Adam. The author took her in hand gently but firmly; he wrote a beautiful poem on the blank page. He breathed on the unopened bud and the flower unfolded. There was a good deal of this, but the critic had learnt agility in a hard school; he skipped several pages and discovered that the author lost his heart to the beautiful savage. (He had known that would happen all along, of course, it didn't need an experienced critic to guess that). They "came together" one night when the Pacific moon shone low in the heavens, mating as purely and innocently as turtle doves.

The critic found the story nauseating in the extreme; it almost made him sick (it might have done so in real earnest if he had had anything to be sick with, but we must remember that he had had no breakfast). He left the manuscript on the table and went to look for the author in the woods.

The author was still sleeping off the effects of his debauch. He was lying flat on his back, breathing loudly and unhygienically through his open mouth. The critic advanced upon him, and shook him into wakefulness with no gentle hand.

"What the devil!" exclaimed the author, sitting up and rubbing his eyes.

"I've read it," said the critic. "I've read it, and it is exactly what I expected —piffle, and sentimental piffle at that."

"It's the best thing I've ever done," declared the author. "A best-seller—beautiful, ideal, romantic. The dew of the morning is upon it."

"Bah!" exclaimed the critic in disgust.

"The public will eat it."

"They won't get the chance."

"You mean—"

"We're here for life," said the critic flatly.

This dreadful thought had not occurred to the author. He had never read a desert island story in which the principals were not eventually rescued by a ship. He considered the matter carefully.

"I might put it into a bottle and throw it into the sea," he said at last. "There's a strong current at the north end of the reef—"

"I shouldn't do that," objected the critic with feigned concern.

"Why not?"

"A shark might swallow it. I'm told that sharks will swallow practically anything."

This was too much. The author rose and walked off into the wood in a dignified manner.

Relations between the two were somewhat strained after this episode—so much so that the author began to wonder whether he had made a mistake in the ending of the story. Was it a love story, or was it a hate story? Did it end with marriage bells or murder? Authors have often felt like murdering critics but no author had ever had such a chance of doing so as this one. It was a chance in a million. The author toyed with the idea for days, and his dislike of the critic grew to alarming proportions. It must be admitted that the author had good reasons for his dislike—not only was the man a soul-less clod, incapable of appreciating a beautiful piece of literature, but he was also a very troublesome and uncongenial companion. He was no help in domestic matters—none at all—and his table manners (if the term be permissible when there is no table) were frankly disgusting. His appearance was going from bad to worse for he had allowed his beard to grow as it pleased. It was straggly and matted—a truly horrible sight. His hair (what there was of it) was long and unkempt, his hands were dirty—and not only his hands.

The author, on the contrary, took a good deal of trouble over his toilet, especially since he had finished the story. He felt it was essential to make a good impression upon the beautiful child of nature when she appeared upon the scenes. It would be simply disastrous to frighten her by looking like a gorilla. So he mended up his clothes as best he could, bathed several times daily, cut his nails and his hair and shaved assiduously with the skeleton's razor. By this time the author was so bound up in his story that he felt it was only a matter of days—or possibly weeks—before the beautiful girl would make her appearance. He was so sure of this that he was not even impatient. The days rolled by—cloudless, golden, warm; they were halcyon days.

One morning when the author was taking his usual swim in the lagoon he was surprised to hear a strange humming sound, very faint and far away. The sound grew louder. He looked up and saw a speck in the sky. The speck increased in size—it was a small bird—it was a large bird—it was an aeroplane.

The author was thrilled to the core; he trembled all over with excitement. He seized his clothes and donned them hastily; he smoothed his hair as best he could and ran to the beach at the other side of the island which was the only possible place for an aeroplane to land.

The aeroplane alighted gracefully upon the coral strand and a slim figure in a leather suit climbed out of the cockpit and stood on the shore lighting a cigarette. The sight was too much for the author who had been smokeless for six whole months.

"For God's sake give me one!" he cried, arriving breathless on the scene.

"Why sure!" agreed the boy—or was it a girl—flicking open a packet of gaspers and tendering a petrol lighter for the author's convenience.

"Ah!" said the author, inhaling the poisonous fumes with blissful enjoyment.

"You've got a nice little place here," remarked the newcomer, taking off the airman's helmet and revealing a shock of red gold curls with which shone like a halo in the rays of the sun.

"Oh!" exclaimed the author. He felt positively dizzy, but whether this was due to the unaccustomed cigarette or the curls it is difficult to say.

"Something the matter?" enquired the girl, shaking out the curls so that the sunbeams leapt and twinkled in their meshes.

"N-no," stammered the author, blinking his eyes.

"That's good," said the girl. "I thought you looked a bit queer. Say, have you got any gasolene handy?"

"Gasolene!"

"Motor spirit," explained the vision casually.

"You mean—you mean that you have run short of petrol!" exclaimed the author in horrified tones.

The girl admitted that this was the case. She gave the author a rapid resume of the circumstances which had landed her so unexpectedly upon the island. He learned that she was a film star of lesser magnitude who had taken up flying as a recreation. She had started out from Los Angeles for a joy ride, had ventured too far and been blown out of her course. She had cruised about for hundreds of miles, and, just as she was beginning to get anxious about her petrol shortage, had sighted the island. There was still a little petrol in the tank, enough for a hundred miles or so, but not enough to feed the engines on their return journey to civilization.

The author now took up the tale and explained to his visitor exactly how he was situated. She listened with shining eyes—it was quite evident that she did not share the critic's distaste for desert islands.

"My!" she exclaimed at last, when the exposition was finished and the author paused, quite out of breath. "My, this is going to put me on the map. I guess this is my lucky day."

The author agreed that the adventure would bring a great deal of desirable publicity, but his natural frankness and probity forced him to disclose the other side of the picture. He pointed out, somewhat diffidently, that things being as they were it was unlikely that his guest would be able to leave the island to make use of the publicity which her adventure would bring.

His diffidence was due to his desire to break the tidings as gently as possible, for he was afraid that his guest would be horror-stricken when the full implication of his words dawned upon her mind. What a dreadful shock for a young girl to learn that she was marooned—possibly for life—upon a desert island. The film star, however, seemed quite unconcerned.

"I guess something will turn up," she remarked placidly, and taking a neat compactum out of the hip pocket of her leather suit she proceeded to powder her nose.

They walked over to the skeleton's hut where the author had, most fortunately, prepared an excellent meal. A couple of parrots, encased in clay, had been left to cook in the glowing embers of the fire. There was also bread-fruit and coconuts. To this repast the film star added a large packet of plain chocolate, and three oranges which she had brought with her in the 'plane.

The sight of the third orange reminded the author that there was another person upon the island—where was the critic? It was most strange that he was not in evidence for he was always ready and waiting for his meals, which made welcome oases in the tedium of his days. The author was surprised and puzzled when he did not appear, but he was also thankful—the man was quite unfit for female society.

The meal was a pleasant one, the author and the film star laughed and chatted like old friends. The author—as has already been seen—was a sentimental man, and he had been starved of women for six months. He was enchanted with his visitor from the skies. It was true that a film star was not the type of girl that he had expected, but that was immaterial. In fact the author—if he had had time to think about the matter—would have been forced to admit that the gods had been extremely good to him. This girl was much better fun than the Child of Nature whose company he had craved.

They had finished their simple but satisfying meal and were lighting cigarettes when a loud buzzing sound broke the silence of the woods.

"Good God, what's that?" cried the author.

He was not left long in doubt as to what the noise signified. An aeroplane soared into sight just over their heads, shaving the tall tops of the coconut palms by a matter of inches.

"Great Snakes, it's my plane!" cried the film star springing to her feet with the agility of an acrobat.

It was indeed her plane. It circled round above their heads, and a small packet, weighted by a stone, dropped into the embers of the fire. The author retrieved the packet, burning his fingers slightly in the process. The film star scarcely noticed, she was gazing upward, her mouth open and her eyes round with astonishment. "My lord!" she said in an awed voice. "My lord! If it isn't a gorilla—a gorilla driving my 'plane!"

The aeroplane banked steeply, climbing higher into the sky, and then bore away across the sea and was lost to view.

"Well," said the film star reflectively. "Well, I guess I've seen most things—but a gorilla driving a plane beats the band."

The author was not listening to her; he was cursing softly beneath his breath, murmuring something about a snake in the grass, a skunk and a female pig.

"Say, is it a *tame* gorilla?" enquired the film star.

"A tame gorilla?"

"That took my plane," she explained.

"It was the critic," replied the author briefly.

The film star's comments on the critic and his immediate forbears were pointed and forceful. The author was obliged to admit that his diatribe was tame and colourless in comparison with hers.

"Well, anyhow, he deserves to drown," said the author at last.

"To drown?" she enquired.

"Yes, when the petrol gives out he will fall into the sea and drown."

"No," said the girl. "At least I mean—well, I guess I'd better own up. There's plenty of juice really"—she had the grace to blush—"I guess it was a dirty trick to play on you," she continued. "It was just—well I had to have some excuse for gate-crashing, hadn't I?"

"Excuse!" cried the author whose susceptible feelings had got the better of him. "Excuse! What a word to use! Angels don't need excuses when they come down from the skies to bestow their company upon lonely shipwrecked mortals—"

"Angels!" she countered. "Why, I guess you've cast me all wrong." And her eyes twinkled at him invitingly.

The author was not slow to avail himself of the invitation. He crushed her in his arms and embraced her with an artistry which was all the more creditable considering that he was so out of practice.

"My!" declared the film star, when at last she could speak. "My, you do know how to kiss—I'll say that for you." Her tones were admiring in the extreme.

It was some little time before they remembered the

packet which had fallen from the aeroplane. When at last they did so, and opened it, they found it to be a letter from the critic. Only a few burnt scraps of the paper remained—

"Humblest apologies . . . impossible to remain . . . situation absolutely impossible to a man of my . . . will send . . ."

They looked at each other and smiled.

"Will send," said the film star, pointing to the words in the message.

"Let's hope he doesn't send too soon!" exclaimed the author fervently.

THE SOFT SPOT

THE SOFT SPOT

1

IT WAS A COLD, STARRY night; snow lay upon the bleak moors in crisp heaps which looked for all the world like piles of bleached linen. The woods were dark, but through the bare branches the stars twinkled and glittered bravely. Two men came silently from among the trees and halted for a few moments looking over the moor. One man stood a little in front of the other as though he were the leader—a short, stocky red-faced individual clothed shabbily in non-descript colours save for a blue handkerchief knotted round his bull neck. He might have been a professional boxer who had come down in the world through his love of the bottle.

His companion was slighter in build and neater in his dress; it would have been hard to guess the man's trade from his face for it was weak and shifty. Truth to tell he had tried his hand at several trades—including motor engineering—and had failed in all. That his new vocation was little to his liking was evinced by the slight shudders which shook him from time to time.

"Are ye feared?" asked his companion, turning and regarding him scornfully. "Ye can gang hame if yer feared."

The other shook his head.

"No Jock, it's the cold—gets into my bones, it does."

"Come away then—we should be seeing the hoose when we're over the rise."

They went on a little way without speaking; the road

which was as hard as iron with the frost made no sound beneath their rubber shod feet.

"Dang the stars!" said the man called Jock. "They're 'maist as bricht as the mune itsel'."

"Maybe it would be better to wait till tomorrow," ventured the other hopefully.

"It's noo or never," Jock replied. "There's only wimmen in the hoose the nicht an' the Major 'ull be hame the morn. Yon Major's unco handy wi' his gun for my liking—Come, Bill, be a man," he added. "Yer no feared o' a pack o' wimmen, are ye?"

Bill did not answer, and the other continued, "Ye would na' go back on me noo wi' the hale thing cut an' dried. Man, think o' the siller—there's eneuch in yon hoose tae keep us baith for a month o' Sabbaths."

"So you say."

"Aye, an' I ken for a fac'. Yon spunes o' the Major's are worth a fortin—MacPhedron said sae an' he kens."

Bill's eyes glittered. He possessed expensive tastes without the means of gratifying them and it was this unfortunate combination which had urged him on the downward path. So far he had kept clear of the law for he had a wholesome dread of its long arm. Tonight was his first departure from the path of honesty and he told himself that it would also be his last. With the money in his pocket—the money promised to him by Jock for his part in the venture—he would be independent. It would be easy to shake himself free from Jock and Co., and to start fresh in a new town or if need be in a new country. Bill was not so enamoured of his own as to be sentimental about leaving it—what had it done for him anyway?

Such were the man's thoughts as he followed his companion over the moors.

"There's the hoose," said Jock at last.

They stood looking down at the house—a long low building of grey stone—which lay below them in a fold of the hills. It was flanked by a sparse wood which shielded it from the prevalent wind.

"Dang the stars!" Jock added softly. "It's unco bricht—we'll need tae work oor way doon through yon wood. What's o'clock?"

"Close on one," was the reply.

Without wasting more time or breath in useless talk Jock set off in an oblique direction gaining cover from the wood. They found a small path and following its windings found themselves after half an hour's walk within a stone's throw of their destination.

"Yon's the dining-room winder," whispered Jock, pointing to a big bow window beside the door. "We'll get in there, the bedrooms face the ither way. Mistress Murray's an' the bairn's."

They crossed the lawn swiftly hardly breathing until they were close to the house, so close that anyone looking from a first floor window could not see them. Here in the shadow of the house Jock unrolled his bundle of tools—each one wrapped carefully in a piece of chamois leather to prevent it rattling—and got busy on the window.

He was very quiet and deft but the slight scrape of the diamond-edged tool cutting the glass brought Bill's heart into his mouth. He cowered against the cold stone, wishing in his craven soul that he had not left the strait way of virtue. It seemed hours until the piece of glass was removed with a piece of putty, the catch of the window lifted and the window opened.

"Stay here," Jock whispered with a contemptuous glance at his confederate. "I'll hand you the siller an' you can put it in the bag—I'm no wantin' Mistress Murray wakened with the rattling o' your teeth."

He swung a leg over the sill and disappeared into the darkness of the room.

2

Major Murray's collection of silver spoons was kept in a glass cabinet which stood in a corner of the room. Jock found the key in a vase which stood on the top of the cabinet; he smiled when the door swung back, it had been so easy.

Jock began to collect the spoons—very carefully for McPhedron had impressed upon him that they were valuable. Suddenly a slight sound disturbed him; he looked up and saw Mrs. Murray standing at the door.

"Can you drive a car?" she said urgently.

He looked at her for a moment, his quick brain groping for some explanation of her words.

Was it a trap, or was she mad?

His pockets were bulging with the Major's spoons; the cabinet was empty.

"Can you drive a car?" repeated Mrs. Murray. "My child is ill and I can't leave him; none of the maids can drive the car—the doctor must be fetched at once. There is no time to be lost."

As if to prove her words there was a low wail, a sound of agony too great to be borne which came from somewhere at the back of the house.

The mother's face blanched at the sound and she wrung her hands.

"Have you no pity, no humanity?" she whispered. "Take what you like, the Major will not grudge you his collection—or if you would rather have money—"

"What's the matter wi' the bairn?" Jock said, grasping the situation.

"I don't know," replied his mother. "The sickness came on a few hours ago and the pain—it may be appendicitis."

"Aye—it may be—or maybe you're fooling me."

"Come up and see him," Mrs. Murray said.

Jock followed her dazedly up the soft carpeted stair. He was calling himself all kinds of a fool but still he went; he was half hypnotised by the strong will of the mother, fighting for her child's life.

They crossed a dimly lit landing and paused for a moment at a door.

"You won't—frighten him?" she whispered.

Jock shook his head.

The child's room was lighted by a lamp which shed a pool of light upon a white table and a small white bed; the rest of the room was a shadow. The burglar moved forward to the bed and stood looking down at the small pathetic figure which lay upon it. There could be no doubt of the truth, for the child's face was grey with pain

29

and he moaned continually.

Mrs. Murray watched the little scene from the door. Hope rose in her breast as she saw the man's face soften; she dug her nails into the palms of her hands and prayed as she had never prayed before.

"Aye," said Jock softly and huskily. "The bairn's needin' the doctor, we maun fetch him."

"Can you drive a car?" Mrs. Murray asked faintly.

"Ma freen' can," replied Jock.

They went downstairs again to the rifled dining-room and, while his hostess found the key of the garage, Jock emptied his pockets and replaced the silver in the cabinet. It seemed to Jock the safest plan, for he was not wanting to meet the doctor with the Major's silver bulging out his pockets. It might lead to awkward questions being asked.

"Ye maun gie me a note tae the doctor," he suggested when Mrs. Murray appeared with the key. She saw the wisdom of this and scrawled a few lines on a scrap of paper.

"Here you are." she said. "Give him this and hurry for God's sake."

3

Jock had been watching her carefully and he felt sure that he could trust her not to betray him. She was safe because there was only one idea in her head. He had had a good deal of experience in his present line of business and in his opinion there were only two sorts of people—those who were frightened of burglars and those who were angry. This woman was neither the one nor the other; the tense anxiety for her child filled her soul to it utmost capacity. There was no room for fear or anger, no energy left to scheme for the protection of her husband's possessions. One thing mattered to her and one only. She was strung like a harp so that a touch set her aquiver; she had lost all sense of values; all idea of time . . .

Jock dropped out of the dining-room window with the key and the letter in his hand. He found his confederate waiting for him, unable to move a step for sheer terror.

It had seemed hours to Bill waiting in the shadow of the house. The wind blew through his clothes and set his teeth chattering yet he dared not leave his post and cross the bright expanse of lawn which lay between him and the woods of safety. His nerves were strung to such a pitch that the sudden appearance of Jock was too much for him, he uttered a shrill scream and swerved across the lawn.

Jock caught his arm and shook him fiercely muttering endearments too lurid for print. The sheer funk of the man was disgusting.

"Pull yourself together," he finished harshly.

"Have you got the stuff?" Bill asked.

"No, an' no likely to," was the reply. "The kid's ill and the house awake—we maun tae Barston for the doctor."

"Are you mad?" cried the younger man swiftly, his dreams of affluence vanishing in the distance.

"Not me," Jock said. He shook off the hand which was clawing his arm and strode across the starlit garden towards the garage. He was wondering secretly what his companion would do, but he knew better than to show any hesitancy. There was only one way to treat the terrified creature and that was to overawe him, to compel him by force of will to obey orders, to sweep him off his feet . . .

When Jock reached the long low building where the Major kept his car he looked back and saw Bill following him.

"Come away," he said. "There's no time tae lose."

They opened the garage doors and ran the four-seater Bean into the yard.

"Get in—ye maun drive like the de'il."

"But Jock—"

"There's nae time tae put off, I'm telling ye. The laddie's deein'—"

"What do I care—"

Bill felt himself lifted and hurled into the driving seat of the car. He crouched there whimpering, beaten. Almost before he knew what he was doing he had touched the self-starter and the car sprang to life.

They swerved out of the yard and went down the straight drive like an arrow from a bow. Once his hands were on the wheel Bill's nervousness left him, for he was completely at home. The car responded to his touch like a living creature recognising its lord and master—the dark woods flashed past.

"Bother the doctor!" said Bill at last. "Let's keep the car, it's better than nothing."

But Jock was seeing something, that small pinched grey

32

face on the pillow rose before his eyes, that low moaning, weak and pitiful, was in his ears.

"We'll get mair out o' it by playing fair," he replied diplomatically.

4

The small town of Barston was wrapped in sleep and the two men had some difficulty in finding the doctor's house. Jock had never felt so desperate in his life; his nerves were all on edge

At last when they were almost in despair the headlights of the Bean shone upon a large brass plate nailed conspicuously to a green gate.

"There's the doc's house," Bill said suddenly.

Jock nodded, he was out of the car before it had come to a stand-still and was pealing the night-bell like a madman.

The doctor's house was square with a flat stone face and no eaves; it was as hideous as a man with no forehead. Dr. Fergus had built on a fine stone porch which sheltered the front door from the wind. It was a great success as far as comfort was concerned but it did not improve the appearance of the building, and his patients were apt to chaff the good doctor about the "nose" which he had given his house. But Dr. Fergus cared little for their chaff as long as he was comfortable, and was fond of quoting that famous saying ascribed to the Iron Duke:

"Give me a man with a nose."

Jock had no eyes for the peculiarities of the house; he was about to ring again when a window on the first floor opened noisily.

"Is it Mistress Macgill's baby?"

The burglar looked up and saw a dark haired man in pink pyjamas.

"It's not. It's the Major's laddie—he's awful bad. Will ye come at once?"

The doctor looked at Jock doubtfully; he was not a prepossessing apparition.

"Why did the Major not come himself?"

"He's away. Mistress Murray had nobody but me tae send. I've a letter for ye."

Doctor Fergus wasted no more time; he shut the window and ran downstairs. A moment later the front door opened and a long thin hand was thrust out.

"The letter, man."

Jock delivered it without a word and then returned to the car to wait for the doctor. He had not long to wait. In an incredibly short time Dr. Fergus came out with a black bag in his hand and threw it into the car.

"Drive like the devil!" he said tersely.

The car bounded forward. The night wind whistled in their ears. The town with its twisting streets was soon left behind; before then stretched the moor road, a pale grey ribbon beneath the stars.

"Will it be appendicitis?" said Jock at last. He had to shout the words for the wind was shrieking through the glass screen like fury.

"How can I tell?"

The doctor was wondering who these men could be—how on earth had the Major's wife managed to discover such a villainous looking pair of scamps to send with the car?

5

Mrs. Murray heard the car in the distance; she was unutterably thankful but not at all surprised. It had never struck her as possible that Jock would fail her; there was something about him which had gained her confidence. She ran down to the door to meet Dr. Fergus so that no time should be wasted.

Dr. Fergus jumped out of the car and followed her into the house without a word. He could see the agony in her face and realised that her need of him was desperate.

The door closed behind him with a bang.

"Now for the spoons," said Bill.

The window of the dining-room was still wide open (for nobody had thought of shutting it) but somehow all zest for the spoons had gone from Jock.

"I'm no feeling like it," he said uncomfortably.

"Well, I am then," replied his confederate, whose nerves had been steadied by the swift run in the powerful car. "I want those spoons. They're ours for the taking."

"Too easy!"

"You're soft," Bill said, slipping out of the driving seat and approaching the window.

Jock watched him climb in and disappear. He was

35

experiencing the feelings of other great leaders; the reins were slipping out of his hands and he could not stop the thing that he had started.

Bill's covetous soul yearned for the spoons and now that there was nothing to fear he meant to have them.

Jock looked up at the stars and he sighed.

"Och well!" he said irresolutely. "I micht as weel have ma share."

And so saying he climbed into the window after his confederate to take part in the sack.

THE SHREW

THE SHREW

Most people who are interested in the affairs of the theatre know the name Gerald Liddell, for it is not many years since "the Great G.L." retired from his long and successful career as a producer of variety entertainment; but public memory is short and few people know—or care to know—that he has retired to his family home in the Borders and is spending the evening of his life in peaceful seclusion.

He is not fit for social gaieties but he enjoys having a few friends to dinner and a chat. It was a piece of luck for me that I happened to be staying with the Reids for some shooting when Mr. Reid received an invitation to dinner at Calderfell House.

"You'd better come, Dickie," said my host. "Edmund Doncaster will be there—and possibly John Macdonald. We're all old fogies compared with you but Gerald Liddell is worth seeing."

"Not *the* Gerald Liddell?" I asked in amazement.

Mr. Reid laughed. "Yes, I suppose you thought G.L. was dead. When famous people retire from theatre business everybody thinks they're dead, but if you come with me tonight you'll see he's still very much alive."

The old lion certainly was worth seeing. I had never set eyes on him before but of course I had seen his portrait in Burlington House and I would have recognised him anywhere. His white curly hair was as thick as ever and, although his face was deeply lined and wrinkled, his eyes were as bright as the eyes of a man half his age. I had heard of his charming manners, and now I saw that the charm still worked. I was the odd man out at the intimate little party (not only a stranger amongst four old friends but also of a different generation) but Sir Gerald welcomed me as if he had known me all my life and put me at ease in a few minutes. I felt the magnetism in him; it was this quality which had brought him his success.

The other two members of the party were interesting too, and the conversation was so stimulating that I scarcely noticed what we ate. After dinner we sat on round the table—a fine old mahogany table discreetly lighted—and the port, which was as mellow as G.L. himself, circulated freely.

I did not say much—it was my place to listen—but my companions had been discussing the misuse of words, and Mr. Doncaster remarked that people often declared themselves to be amazed or dumbfounded when in reality they were no more than surprised.

"Have you ever been dumbfounded?" asked G.L. looking round the table at his guests. "Have you ever lost the power of speech through astonishment? I don't mean fear—that's different."

The others were silent for a few moments.

"I can't remember an occasion off-hand," said Mr. Doncaster at last.

"Have you, sir?" I asked eagerly.

Sir Gerald nodded. "I can remember one occasion when I was literally dumbfounded."

Of course we all clamoured for the story and after a

good deal of persuasion he consented to tell it.

"Well, don't blame me if it doesn't come up to your expectations," he warned us. "It was a long time ago and I wasn't so tough. Pass the port, Dickie. It always seems to come to a halt beside you."

I did as I was told. The fact was I was too interested in the conversation to remember to pass the port. There was a short silence, while Sir Gerald marshalled his thoughts and then he began his story.

"You're all too young to remember a Variety Entertainment called *Youth at the Prow*. It was the first big variety entertainment that I produced on my own. Nowadays it would be called a Revue, of course, but in those days we just called it Variety. I don't mind admitting that *Youth at the Prow* gave me a few sleepless nights before it got going for it just had to be a success. I knew that if it failed I was bust. I was determined that the show should go with a swing; I was determined that it should be 'different': I went about all over the country looking for new talent.

"Somebody told me there was a ventriloquist called Victor Blunt appearing at Leeds so I went down from London to have a look at him. I told nobody I was going because I didn't want him to know I was there, but unfortunately someone recognised me and told him. It was all the more unfortunate because I decided that he wouldn't do at all, the act was far too slight and Blunt himself wasn't up to London standards. It was a pity, but it couldn't be helped. I was coming out of the theatre when

41

Blunt ran after me and asked anxiously if I would give him an audition in London. He explained that he had been nervous and had not been able to do himself justice, and added that the acoustics of the theatre were bad—all the usual excuses for a poor performance! The fellow seemed pretty desperate; in fact he looked down and out, and I was sorry for him, but it was useless to raise his hopes so I told him quite plainly that it was no good. Then I went back to the hotel and packed and took a taxi to the station.

"It was a horrible night, cold and raw, and there was a thick yellow fog, the sort of fog with a nasty taste to it, so I wasn't surprised to find that the train to London was over an hour late. The waiting room was very badly lighted but there was a good fire of soft coal blazing cheerfully in the grate. Beside the fire a man was sitting— it was Victor Blunt.

"Blunt rose when I went in and offered me his chair but I drew up another chair and sat down. I was rather annoyed for I thought Blunt had pursued me to the station to have another try . . . but he explained that he was in the same predicament as myself and was waiting for the train.

" 'It's seventy minutes late,' said Blunt in a low voice. 'It's very unfortunate because my wife isn't feeling well.' He glanced across the room as he spoke and I saw she was lying on a sofa; one of those hard horsehair sofas they have in station waiting-rooms. She was covered with a rug and there was a shawl round her head. The light was so bad that I had not noticed there was anyone there until

Blunt mentioned her.

" 'She doesn't look very comfortable,' I said, lowering my voice.

" 'She's asleep,' said Blunt.

" 'I'm not asleep,' said Mrs. Blunt peevishly. 'Nobody could sleep with people coming in and out and all this noise going on.'

"It was noisy, of course. Porters were shouting at each other and rolling heavy barrows along the platform and trains were being shunted to and fro.

" 'Are you warm enough, Elsie?' Blunt asked.

" 'What's the use of asking?' she exclaimed. 'We've only got the one rug. We shouldn't have come tonight in this horrible fog. We should have waited until tomorrow. I told you that, but you wouldn't listen.'

"Blunt took off his overcoat and going over to his wife he tucked it round her. 'There, that's better, isn't it?' he said.

" 'Well, don't blame me if you get a chill,' she replied. 'And don't stand there gazing at me.'

"The wretched man came back to the fire and sat down with his head in his hands.

" 'Look here,' I said in a low voice. 'Do you think Mrs. Blunt would like a cup of tea? I might be able to get one for her in the restaurant.'

"Blunt looked up and smiled gratefully. 'It's very kind of you, sir. I believe it might do her good – ' He raised his voice. 'Would you like a cup of tea, Elsie?' he asked her.

" 'No, I wouldn't,' she replied crossly. 'Railway tea isn't worth drinking. It would probably make me sick.'

" 'I'm sorry, Mr. Liddell,' whispered Blunt. 'When she isn't feeling well she's a bit—difficult.'

"Difficult was scarcely the word! However it was none of my business so I murmured that I understood and it didn't matter at all.

" 'What are you whispering about Victor?' demanded Mrs. Blunt. 'I suppose you're complaining about me. You're always complaining about me to other people behind my back.'

"He tried to stop her. 'Elsie, this gentleman is Mr. Gerald Liddell,' he said in a warning tone.

" 'Oh—' she said doubtfully. 'Oh well, what does it matter? He's turned you down, hasn't he? He told you that you weren't any good. I've told you the same thing over and over again but you wouldn't believe me. Perhaps you'll believe the great Mr. Gerald Liddell.' She added bitterly, 'Perhaps you'll stop all this nonsense and get a useful job which will bring in a little money.'

" 'We can discuss that later,' said Blunt miserably. 'This isn't the time or the place to discuss our private affairs.'

"I felt very sorry for the man; it even crossed my mind to give him a trial, but I wasn't producing *Youth at the Prow* for fun. I simply couldn't afford to be charitable.

" 'That's just like you!'" Mrs. Blunt told her unfortunate husband. 'You're always putting things off. We'll discuss it here and now. I tell you I'm sick of pinching and scraping and trailing all over the country and living in wretched lodgings. I never would have married you if I'd known what I was letting myself in for. I want a home of my own—'

" 'Elsie—please!' exclaimed Blunt. 'I've told you we'll discuss it later. You're making Mr. Liddell feel very uncomfortable. Please be quiet!'

"It certainly was most unpleasant for me. I rose and walked over to the door murmuring something about seeing whether the train was coming. It was cold and foggy outside but I felt I would rather walk up and down the platform than be mixed up in a matrimonial dispute.

" 'I won't be quiet!' cried Mrs. Blunt, her voice rising hysterically. 'I shall say what I like! I don't care who hears me! I'm just about fed up with you—'

"Blunt had been very patient, but it seemed that his patience had limits. He leapt to his feet and advanced towards her threateningly. 'And I'm fed up with you,' he declared. 'If you don't hold your tongue I'll make you!'

"By this time I was at the door with my hand on the door handle, but when the woman let out a piercing scream I turned involuntarily.

"Blunt was standing beside the sofa shaking out the rug. The woman had disappeared."

Sir Gerald paused and looked round the table with a mischievous smile on his lips. He certainly had a sense of theatre.

"Disappeared!" exclaimed Mr. Reid incredulously. "What do you mean?"

"I mean she had vanished," said Sir Gerald, holding out his hands and raising his eyebrows. "She just wasn't there."

"Where was she, G.L.?" asked Mr. Macdonald in

surprise.

"That was what I wanted to know," said Sir Gerald. "The waiting-room was bare—there was no place to hide a cat—and I had been standing at the only exit.

"I looked at Blunt and saw that he was smiling. 'It's all right, Mr. Liddell,' he said. 'You can come back and sit by the fire in peace. Elsie won't bother us any more.'

" 'But—where is she?' I exclaimed in bewilderment.

" 'Nowhere,' he replied. 'Elsie doesn't exist.'

" 'Doesn't exist!' I echoed.

" 'There's no Elsie,' explained Blunt. 'I haven't got a wife, Mr. Liddell. There was just my suitcase on the sofa and the thermos basket covered with the rug and a shawl. You can see for yourself.'

"I was literally dumbfounded. You see the woman was so real to me. Her querulous voice and her rudeness and selfishness had built up in my mind a definite personality —the personality of a shrew. She was so real that I felt I could have recognised her in the street. It was absolutely incredible that she did not exist and had never existed. I don't know how long I stood there gaping.

" 'I won't be quiet! I shall say what I like!' exclaimed Elsie's voice from the chair beside the fire.

"I swung round hastily and looked at the chair: it was empty, of course. Then the spell was broken and I began to laugh.

" 'I'm sorry, Mr. Liddell,' said Blunt. 'It's very good of you to take it like this. I wasn't sure whether you would be angry or not but I knew you had a sense of humour— so I risked it. You see I was desperate.' "

Sir Gerald paused again and smiled in a thoughtful manner.

"Well, there isn't much more to tell you," he said. "Of course, I booked Blunt then and there for *Youth at the Prow* and we put on the little sketch exactly as it had happened, the grim station-waiting-room and all. I acted in it as myself, but I don't think I ever acted the part so convincingly as the first time."

"I wish I could have seen it," I told him.

"But it wasn't a success, you know," said Sir Gerald reminiscently. "It didn't come off on the stage. You see ninety per cent of the audience thought it was a disappearing trick—the vanishing lady! Some people declared they had seen a panel in the wall open and the woman slide through."

"They missed the point completely!" Mr. Doncaster exclaimed.

"Yes, they missed the point," nodded Sir Gerald. "I suppose one couldn't blame them (stages are known to have hidden panels and trap-doors, station waiting-rooms haven't) but I never regretted booking Victor Blunt for the Show. He was the best ventriloquist I ever heard. When we realised the sketch had misfired we turned it into a burlesque—with Elsie's voice coming from different corners of the room there wasn't much subtlety about it, but it brought down the House. That's the way things happen in theatre business. Pass the port, Dickie."

THE MILLINER
OF
AUCHENTOSHAN

THE MILLINER OF AUCHENTOSHAN

SCENE

The Milliners shop. There are two doors. Several tables with stands upon them upon which hats are displayed. A dressing-table with mirror and a hand mirror. Several chairs. A chest of drawers (or box) with hats in it.

ENTER <u>MRS. SWAN</u> *(a customer). She is middle-aged and nicely dressed. She looks round, surprised to find nobody there. She looks at the door leading to the back premises. She looks at the hats but does not touch them.*

MRS SWAN: *Coughing to attract attention.* Ahem! *Nobody appears.*

MRS SWAN: *At last makes up her mind to rap on the door. Raps rather timidly.* Is anyone there?

ENTER <u>MISS MACNAPESTRY</u> *(the milliner).*

MISS MAC: Were ye wantin' somethin'?

MRS SWAN: Yes, I wanted a hat. Are you—

MISS MAC: *In surprise:* A hat! What would ye be wantin' it for?

MRS SWAN: *Astounded.* What for? To wear, of course.

MISS MAC: Yon hat ye've got on is guid enough.
              There's a lot of wear in it yet.

MRS SWAN: I'm going, to a wedding tomorrow, so I
              want something smart.

MISS MAC: Och, that'll be Jamie Macfee's marriage.
              He's tae be married the morn. I'm weal
              acquainted wit the Macfees, ye ken. Ma
              mither wis a Balfour and her step-faither's
              brither married Mistress Macfee's cousin.

MRS SWAN: *Bewildered:* Oh—I see.

MISS MAC: *Shaking her head:* He was an awfu' man.
              He was neather tae hand nor tae bind. An
              awfu' time she had wi' him, puir body.

MRS SWAN: How dreadful.

MISS MAC: Aye, it was that—but he didna' live lang—
              that was one comfort. He was taken in his
              prime.

MRS SWAN: *Trying to get back to business:* Er—what
              about a hat?

MISS MAC: *Does not reply. Looks surprised.*

MRS SWAN: Oh. Perhaps—perhaps the milliner is out.

MISS MAC: There's naeboy here but me.
             Macnapestry's the name.

MRS SWAN: Oh. Well, Mrs Macnapestry, I want a hat.

MISS MAC: I'm a Miss.

MRS SWAN: *Puzzled:* A Miss?

MISS MAC: *Smiling grimly:* I missed me chance.

MRS SWAN: What chance? I don't understand.

MISS MAC: The chance tae get married. Tae tell ye the
             plain truth I never wanted a man. I'm well
             enough as I am.

MRS SWAN: *After a slight pause:* You *do* sell hats, don't
             you?

MRS MAC: *Grimly:* Whiles. There's some folk are just
             awfu' extravagant, they come here wantin'
             a new hat when there's naethin' wrong wi'
             their auld yin.

MRS SWAN: *Apologetically:* But I'm going to a wedding
             so I must have a new hat. *Looks round and
             points.* What about that one?

MISS MAC: *Not moving:* Ooh, ye wouldna' suit it.

53

MRS SWAN: Or that one.

MISS MAC: Och, I couldna' recommend yon hat. It's an awfu' queer colour. Ye'd not have anything ye could wear wi' it.

MRS SWAN: May I try it on? *Sits down at the mirror.*

MISS MAC: *Gets it very reluctantly and crams it on to her head.* Och, it's no' the thing at all.

MRS SWAN: *Arranging it:* I don't think it's at all bad, really. I could have a feather in it, perhaps.

MISS MAC: A feather! Whet would ye be wantin' wi' a feather?

MRS SWAN: Just to smarten it up a bit.

MISS MAC: It would luik rideeckulous.

MRS SWAN: Let me try that one - the blue one.

MISS MAC: *Suddenly stands still and listens.* Whaesht, what's that: *Rushes from room, holding her head and calling out.* Och, maircy, it's ma heid!

MRS SWAN: *Half rises and then hesitates. Does not know what to do.*

MISS MAC: *Returning:* It was ma heid.

MRS SWAN: *Sympathetically:* I'm so sorry. Perhaps you
               would like to go and lie down. I could
               come back later.

MISS MAC: *Surprised:* Lie down! There's neathin' the
               matter wi' me.

MRS SWAN: I thought you said—

MISS MAC: Ma heid wis biling over, that's all.

MRS SWAN: Boiling over! *She looks horrified.*

MISS MAC: There's nee hairm done. I've turned doon
               the gas.

MRS SWAN: Oh, a sheep's head!

MISS MAC: Aye, I got the flesher tae singe it. Some
               folk prefair hough for broth, but I prefair
               heid.

MRS SWAN: *Losing patience:* Miss Macnapestry, I want
               a hat.

MISS MAC: Umphm, so ye said.

MRS SWAN: Have you anything that would suit me?

MISS MAC:	No a thing. Ye'll just need tee wear yer auld yin.
MRS SWAN:	What about that red one?
MISS MAC:	*Takes it down reluctantly*: Och, it's a silly wee hat an' no worth the money. *Crams it on her head.* Ye could never wear it, that's certain.
MRS SWAN:	Why not? *Turns her head and uses hand mirror.*
MISS MAC	*Grimly:* Folk would laugh.
MRS SWAN:	*Removing hat quickly:* Let me try that one, please.
MISS MAC:	*Scornfully:* Yon! It wouldna' be guid enough for a marriage.
MRS SWAN:	May I try it on?
MISS MAC:	*Cramming it on her head:* There, what did I tell ye: moir like a funeral in my opeenion.
MRS SWAN:	No, it isn't so good. The red one is the best, so far. *Puts on the red.* It really is *quite* nice.

MISS MAC: It's just a mess. I'm wonderin' why I ever took it fra' the traveller. Sich a colour ae it is! *Snatches it off.* If ye maun hae a hat ye'd better wi' yon broon one. It wouldna' be sae conspeeckuous. *Gives it to her.*

MRS SWAN: *Takes it and puts it on:* Rather dowdy, I think.

MISS MAC: *Gleefully:* Aye, ut's dowdy, right enough. Ye luik like an auld tattle-wife.

MRS $WAN: *Takes it off quickly and puts on another:* No, the brim is too wide.

MISS MAC: It's no sae bad, mind you. It's the best yet.

MRS SWAN: Do you think so—really? *Turns her head.*

MISS MAC: Aye, it hides your face better nor the others.

MRS SWAN: What about that green one?

MISS MAC: Ye'd never wear green tae a marriage!

MRS SWAN;   *Hopelessly:* It seems hopeless!

MISS MAC: Aye, it does so. Ye'd be better tae give up the idea, I'm thinking.

MRS SWAN: Do you ever sell a hat, Miss Macnapestry?

MISS MAC: *Sadly:* Whiles I dae.

MRS SWAN: That *is* surprising.

MISS MAC: *Sighing:* Some folks are gey stubborn.

MRS SWAN;   They must be.

MISS MAC: Some folks dinna ken whit's guid for them.

MRS SWAN: It's good to have a new hat sometimes. It's a sort of tonic. It gives one confidence—at least it usually does.

MISS MAC: *Incredulously:* I never haird *that.*

MRS SWAN: No, I daresay not. *She sighs.*

MISS MAC: *Triumphantly:* It wasna' much of a *tonic* tae Mistress MacWhirter.

MRS SWAN: Did she buy a hat from you?

MISS MAC: She did so. It was an awfu' like thing but she was gey taken up wi' it and naethin' would turn her. I tellt her it was a piece of extravagance but she didna' heed.

MRS SWAN: Perhaps it wasn't an extravagance—

MISS MAC: Aye, but it was. She wore it away an' she
             wore it tae the kirk, but she'll never wear
             it again.

MRS SWAN: What nonsense! You can't possibly know
             that.

MISS MAC: *Gravely:* The wumman's deid.

             Mrs Swan is dumbfounded.

MISS MAC: *After a pause:*
             She'll no need a hat where she's gone. It's
             a croon she's wearin'—mebbe. *Pause.*
             Saxteen shillins' and elevenpence she paid
             for it, too.

MRS SWAN: Did she die—very suddenly?

MISS MAC: *Nodding portentously:* She was taken in a
             flash. At one moment she was in this
             wurrld, supping her parriten and the next
             she was away. Deith is no respecter of
             pairsons.

MRS SWAN: No, but perhaps—

MISS MAC: There's nane o' us can tell oor end.

MRS SWAN: *Shudders:* That's true. *She hesitates and then pulls herself together.* I think I like the red hat best. *Puts it on.*

MISS MAC: Ye're luikin' a wee bit peelie-wallie. Maybe it's the colour. It's an awfu' tryin' colour, reed.

MRS SWAN: *Firmly:* How much is it?

MISS MAC: *Triumphantly.* It's seventeen an' nine— ye'd never pay that for it.

MRS SWAN: I don't think it's out of the way. *Takes out her purse.*

MISS MAC: If ye maun ha'e a hat ye'd be better wi' yon broon yin. It's twelve an' three.

MRS.SWAN: I don't care for it at all.

MISS MAC: Nor me—but it's cheaper.

MRS SWAN: I'd rather have this one, thank you.

MISS MAC: It luiks awfu' queer on ye, somehoo.

MRS SWAN: Seventeen and nine. *Holds out the money.*

MISS MAC: I canna wrap it. The cat had kittens in the paper.

MRS SWAN: Oh, I never expected you to wrap it. I'll just wear it.

MISS MAC: *Taking the money reluctantly, counting it.* Aye, that's right. Ye'd best wear it to get it into the sit o' yer held. It's a queer shape.

MRS SWAN: *Making for the door.* Goodbye, Mss Macnapestry.

MISS MAC: Guid day tae ye. I'm real glad I was able tae help ye.

CURTAIN

MISTER MCGIBBON'S
DAUGHTER

MISTER McGIBBON'S
DAUGHTER

Mister McGibbon was a railway porter;
He had a wifie and an only daughter.
Maud was a miracle of grace and beauty
But, with it all, was never never snooty.
She was the moon and stars to the McGibbons;
They bought her lovely clothes and coloured ribbons;
  Maudie was better far than television
  (At least this was her parents' firm decision).

Unluckily the clothes that suited Maudie
Were the expensive, not the cheap and gaudy.
In flowing model gowns and real chinchilla
Maudie McGibbon was an absolute killer.
And so (it was not really very funny)
Garments for Maudie cost a lot of money.
  McGibbon gave up beer and fags and snuff
  But even so they hadn't got enough.

Things went from bad to worse, from hard to harder
Till there was literally nothing in the larder;
Then Mr. M. (to keep their tums from gurgling)
Decided he must do a spot of burgling.
And, studying the matter at his leisure,
Resolved to bag the Duke of Gantry's treasure
    And, since he did not want to take a stranger,
    Maud volunteered to help and share the danger.

Choosing a night of foul and foggy weather
The two adventurers set out together.
Maudie had dressed with care, and looked a pet
In gorgeous furs and eau-de-nil georgette.
She knew her part, she'd had her clear instructions:
"You vamp the Duke, but vanish if there's ructions."
    And Maud had promised she would do her best
    To carry out her parent's wise behest.

In silence they approached the House of Gantry
And entered by a window in the pantry.
McGibbon's plans were so well-laid, so clever,
They had no difficulties whatsoever.
Maud entertained the Duke with some tomfoolery
While her papa levanted with the jewellery.
    The whole affair went off without a hitch
    It *was* an easy way of getting rich.

The burglary occasioned a sensation
And every daily rag in circulation
Came out with headlines: *Ducal Mansion Robbery!*
In fact there was the usual fuss and bobbery.
Detectives combed the house from roof to cellar
Without avail; they could not trace the feller
    Into thin air he'd vanished with his plunder;
    It was a mystery, a nine days wonder.

Meanwhile the Duke (quite young and rather stupid)
Had fallen victim to the darts of Cupid.
What time McGibbon bagged his diamond lockets
And with tiaras filled capacious pockets,
Maud played her part in such a charming fashion
She kindled in his heart a fatal passion.
    "Oh Maudie, be my duchess!" thus he pleaded —
    It was the very thing that Maudie needed.

From childhood it had been her great ambition
To wear a bridal dress of long tradition,
A wreath of orange-blossom on her curls,
A veil of lace and softly gleaming pearls;
What's more the dreams of this attractive spinster
Were centred on St. Margaret's, Westminster . . .
    This being so (it scarcely needs narration)
    She murmured "Yes" without much hesitation.

And now we reach the highlight of the story:
'Tis Maudie's wedding day, her Day of Glory.
Guests come in hundreds; champagne flows like
                                                        water;
The sun shines golden on McGibbon's daughter.
The streets are thronged with wildly cheering people
And wedding-bells chime gaily from the steeple.
   The marriage is so splendid, so romantic
   Those who have not been asked are simply frantic.

Maud's parents (once the marriage feast was over)
Took the Blue Train and crossed the sea at Dover;
They travelled on the Continent at leisure
Upon the proceeds of the stolen treasure.
And, though they missed their girlie very much,
They knew that she was "born to be a Dutch".
   Meanwhile the bridal pair flew to Havana
   And honeymooned in a delirious manner.

The Duchess long retained her peerless beauty
And, what is more important, did her duty:
She wore her coronet with style and grace
And bore twin sons to carry on the race.
Duchess Brings Off a Double screamed the papers.
(How Maudie chuckled at their silly capers!)
   And so my story ends with joy and laughter,
   Maud and her Duke were happy ever after.

STORING THE HEAT
OF THE SUN

STORING THE HEAT OF THE SUN

"THE DREAMS OF TODAY are the achievements of tomorrow," said Sir Ebury Barton as he filled his glass and passed the port to his left hand neighbour.

There were half a dozen of us dining with him that night and the talk had been fast and furious, but Sir Ebury's words fell into a little silence and we all looked up.

"Don't mind me," he said. "I was only being sententious."

"Please go on, Sir," said Ruddridge, a young naval officer who had just got his lieutenant's badge and was as bashful about it as a debutante.

"I was under the impression that I had finished," said Sir Ebury smiling.

"Then the dreamers are ahead of the doers," said Clapperton incredulously. We laughed at that for Clapperton was a materialist with no room in his well-balanced well-stuffed head for such things as dreams.

"Miles ahead," nodded Sir Ebury. "What ails fifty per cent of the inmates of our lunatic asylums save that they have been born out of time?"

"You mean if they had been born say fifty years later they would have been sane?"

"Something like that," was the laughing reply.

"Oho!" cried Ruddridge. "There's a good yarn at the back of this or I'm a Dutchman."

The dinner had been excellent and the wine was to

match, which is to say that we were all in the mood for a good yarn, as Ruddridge put it, and after a little persuasion our host agreed to spin it.

"Your blood be upon your own heads if you are bored to death," he said, settling himself in his big oak chair and leaning one elbow on the arm. "The thing is hardly a yarn —merely one of those queer incidents that open up vistas to the imagination. Some years ago I was doing a walking tour in the West Country. I was taking it easily for it was hot weather and I was in no particular hurry to get anywhere. I used to get up early and do about ten miles and then rest until the sun went down and do a bit more. One day—the hottest of all, a perfect boiler—I fell asleep under a tree in a field beside the road. I must have slept for about an hour; when I woke I had the feeling that somebody was looking at me—you know the feeling. I looked round and there, sure enough, was a man sitting quite near me staring at me intently.

"I was still half asleep and we gazed at each other for a few moments without speaking. He was quite a well-dressed man but a trifle shabby. His blue suit was well cut, but it had seen its best days and his shoes had the same appearance of having come down in the world. The man's face, however, was quite different from what we usually associate with those who have been left behind in the race of life. It was neither haggard with want not sodden with drink. It was a sound shining face (don't laugh, haven't you seen a boy's face shine when he knows you are going to tip him?) His eyes were blue and the brooding inward look of a visionary, his hair was blown and rather untidy and he had no hat.

" 'Good afternoon,' he said in a pleasant educated voice. 'I have been watching you for some time.'

"Now it is rather annoying to be told that somebody has been watching you sleeping, especially in the middle of the day. Whether it is because one does not look one's best on these occasions or because of a primitive instinct—the fear of being in a helpless condition—I don't know, but for some reason I did not feel angry with this man. He seemed not to come under ordinary laws. I can't explain what I mean—he seemed aloof from the world, as if he did not belong to the world. Yet he was obviously enjoying it. His face was full of happiness, friendliness and content.

" 'It's good to be out on a day like this,' he said, and in these words I thought I had found the clue to his oddness. He was probably a city worker and had come to the country for a day's outing.

" 'Aren't you afraid of getting sunstroke?' I asked him.

"He shook his head and laughed happily.

" 'The sun will not hurt me. I am storing up every ray of it in my body.'

The speech would not cause any surprise now, when every man in the street knows something of the curative properties of the sunshine, but this incident occurred some years ago, before the medical profession had fully awakened to the new ideas. I confess I was interested.

" 'Everything stores sunshine,' he continued, more as if he were talking to himself than to me. 'The whole world is a vast storage house—feel that stone,' he added suddenly, leaning forward and placing a large pebble in my hands.

" 'It is very hot,' I said stupidly.

" 'Of course it is hot,' he cried. 'It has been lying in the sun for hours—is it still hot?'

" 'Yes.'

" 'Well, it's not in the sun now, is it? Therefore, it has stored up the sun's heat.'

"He was leaning forward now, expounding his argument, and his blue eyes were no longer brooding, they were blazing. 'Sermons in stones—there's one for you, sir.'

" 'You mean—' I began.

" 'I mean just this. In a few years time—ten or fifty, what does it matter—you will be scrapping all that complicated gas and coal and electric heating of yours. Why? Because there will be no need for it. We shall store the heat of the sun during the day and use it when and where we need it.'

"I said it seemed a visionary's dream.

" 'Dream!' he said. 'What were aeroplanes and wireless to our grandfathers? Sir, the dreams of today are the achievements of tomorrow.'

" 'It would be a difficult problem to solve,' I suggested.

" 'Problems are here to be solved,' was the swift reply. 'I can't understand why it hasn't been solved before. Isn't it more easily understood than wireless? Isn't it more sensible? More necessary? Isn't heat the foremost need of man?'

"I suppose he saw that I was interested for he took a

small phial out of his pocket and handed it to me.

" 'There,' he said. 'That is the foundation stone of the World's Sun Store. My life has not been all spent in dreaming; there has been hard work too. Years of work, years of failures and disappointments, and now at last a small modicum of success. Just enough success to show that I am on the right path, just enough to urge me on to further efforts for the good of mankind.'

" 'What is this?' I asked him, looking at the small bottle with great curiosity.

" 'Listen to me and then tell me that I am a visionary of you like. That phial contains a fixing solution—I will not trouble you with the chemical details of its contents—enough to say that a stone treated with this mixture will retain its sun heat for twice as long as another stone. Not much use perhaps, but it shows that I am on the right path, shows that the thing is possible—if I can do that much, I can do more.'

"His enthusiasm was infectious.

" 'Take a stone heated by the sun and fixed hot—in much the same way as a photograph is fixed—with my solution. What could you use it for? Put it in a bath of cold water overnight and next morning plunge into water heated by the sun's own rays. Put a dozen of them in you room and do away with fires—keep your food hot—air your bed—why, there is no end to its uses.'

" 'And this solution of yours actually causes the stone to retain the heat of the sun?' I asked him.

" 'Actually does,' he replied. 'Though of course not to a degree that can be of any use—you understand that? My invention is merely at the experimental stage. Come sir, you are interested. Take two stones—here they are. Now I will pour some of my fixing solution on one of them. We will leave both in the sun for five minutes so that they may absorb the rays equally, then we will place them both in the shade for another five minutes before marking the test. What do you say?'

"I replied that I was willing to watch the experiment, as indeed I was for the man's manner was convincing. His eyes shone with excitement as he uncorked his precious bottle and poured some of the greenish yellow liquid onto one of the stones, rubbing it in well with his fingers. He then found a rock conveniently near and placed the two stones upon it so that each should get its fair share of sunlight. He borrowed my watch to time his experiment and sat down as patiently as he could to wait for five minutes.

" 'Five minutes in the sun and then five minutes in the shade,' he said, rubbing his hands together with satisfaction. 'I feel sure I shall be able to convince you of the importance of my discovery. I have a thermometer here so that there shall be no mistake about the temperature.' "

"And what was the result?" asked Ruddridge eagerly, for Sir Ebury had stopped to light a long cigar.

"I'm afraid to tell you," replied out host, smiling, "for fear that you will think I am romancing. There could be no doubt whatever that after five minutes in the shade, the stone which had been treated with the fixing solution was still quite hot, and the other one stone cold."

He smiled at his joke and looked round the table to see what we were making of the tale.

"There was no possibility of —" somebody ventured.

"None whatever," replied Sir Ebury. "I watched him like a hawk the whole time—and besides that, he was interested in the experiment himself, which he would not have been if the thing had been a hoax."

" 'And if heat, why not light also?' said the experimenter at last when we had tested the stone by every means in our power. 'Why shouldn't we store light in the same way? Think of the convenience of roads absorbing the light of the sun all day and giving it out all night—the saving of electricity. Think of light in the home—pure rays of sunshine absorbed by stones in the garden and brought in to illuminate the whole place without one penny of cost save the small initial outlay on the fixing solution.'

" 'That would surely be much more difficult,' I said.

" 'Difficult, perhaps, but not impossible,' he replied slowly, and once more his eyes took on that inward brooding look.

"By this time the sun was setting and I realised that if I wanted to get to my destination that night it was time to be making a move. I shook hands with my fellow experimenter and wished him luck.

" 'If I don't get it, somebody will,' he said cheerfully, "and so long as the problem is solved, I don't mind.'

"I had gone about a mile, my mind still full of my strange experience, when I suddenly remembered that I had left my watch lying on the rock where the experiment had taken place. I went back at once, for the watch was a valuable one, but neither it nor my friend were to be seen. Probably he had found it after I had gone and not knowing my name would take it to the nearest police station. I had only to leave my name and address and have it forwarded to me.

"Once more I set off, walking quickly to make up for lost time, and very soon I came to a typical little country police station with a typical country police sergeant leaning over the garden wall smoking an old briar pipe.

" 'Good evening, sergeant,' I said. "I want you to help me to recover my watch. I left it about three miles back lying on a stone and when I went back it had gone. It seems a very foolish thing to have done—'

" 'It does,' he said, looking at me in a queer way. 'You wasn't by any chance engaged on a scientific experiment at the time, was you?'

"I suppose I looked the amazement that I felt.

" 'Well well!' he said. 'Well I never—it's not for me to say you did a foolish thing for I did the same myself not a week ago, and I've not seen my watch since and not likely to neither—Collins!' he called, turning his head and beckoning to a man who was digging in the garden. 'Collins, here's Sunshine Smith got loose again and pinched this gentleman's watch same as he did mine.'

"Collins stuck his spade into the ground and came across the potatoes to the wall. His boots and trousers proclaimed him one of the Force but he had thrown off his blue tunic on account of the heat.

" 'Well I'll be blowed!' he said weightily.

" 'What do you mean? Is the man an impostor?' I asked, looking from one to the other in surprise.

" 'Well, is he?' said the sergeant. 'That's just what I'm wanting to know myself. They've got him locked up as a lunatic—when he doesn't escape, that is—and he's certainly got a liking for other folks' watches, but whether he's an impostor or not—' He rubbed the back of his head and looked at me with comic bewilderment. 'Those stones now, it's queer, isn't it sir? But perhaps you'll be wanting to make a deposition against him—'

"He got his notebook out of his pocket, a trifle unwillingly it seemed to me.

" 'What about *your* watch?' I asked him, for I felt sure that there was something more in this than met the eye.

" 'Well, sir, I didn't do nothing about it,' he replied apologetically. 'You see it was only a cheap one after all, an' somehow I felt I'd got my money's worth out of him. I shouldn't have like to think of him in jug on my account, and him liking the sunshine so much … But your watch'll be a valuable one no doubt.'

" 'No,' I said slowly. 'No, I think I got my money's worth too—so goodnight to you.'

" 'Goodnight, sir,' replied the sergeant, shutting up his notebook and restoring it to his pocket with alacrity.

"I looked back as I went down the road and I saw that Collins had gone back to his digging, but the very human sergeant was looking up at the sun and then feeling the warm stones of the wall with the same bewildered expression on his round fat face."

"And what next?" we all asked as Sir Ebury stopped

speaking.

"Nothing next," he replied with a laugh. "I never saw nor heard anythink of Sunshine Smith or my £30 chronometer again. And I can't tell you to this day whether the fellow was an unconscionable rogue or a man born out of his time. But I couldn't help feeling that someday—somehow—"

He broke off and held up his glass of ruby port to the light.

"Look at the sunbeams imprisoned in this glass of wine —Well, here's to Sunshine Smith and the achievements of tomorrow!"

TWO WISHES

TWO WISHES

1

The new golf course at Greenfell was under the management of a very up-to-date syndicate who were determined to run it on new lines. Its amenities were advertised on every hoarding by gaily coloured posters and persuasive letter-press. Port Andrew looked on and smiled—it knew all there was to know about golf and did not approve of innovations. Golf was golf, and like good wine, it required no bush. What did Greenfell want with a course of its own when Port Andrew with its high traditions and deep bunkers was only two miles away?

In spite of its scorn, however, Port Andrew found in the Greenfell Golf Course an inexhaustible subject of conversation. They were talking about it in the Ladies' Club one morning when Mary Douglas strolled in after her round.

"What is the latest?" she asked, smiling down at the little group in the wicker chairs.

Half a dozen voices enlightened her.

"They are going to have a woman professional! Two hundred a year and a house—only championship players need apply—here's the paper about it—did you ever hear of such a thing – "

Mary took the paper from her friend and read it carefully. She was a fair-haired, blue-eyed girl, small but well-proportioned with a frank cheerful face. At the moment, however, there was a frown of concentration between her straight brows.

"May I keep this paper?" she said. "I'm rather interested."

"Are you thinking of applying for the job, Mary?" asked Dora Inglis, laughing.

"Yes, I am," replied Mary seriously. "I wouldn't mind the job at all, and that little bungalow is very attractive. The money would be a great help to mother and me. Things have gone rather badly lately, you see, and to tell you the truth I've been wondering what I *could* do. An office life does not appeal to me, besides, I'm no use at figures—"

The other girls stopped laughing and murmured. They all liked Mary; she played a good game of golf and was a thorough little sport.

"Of course there will be lots of applications," she continued thoughtfully, "but perhaps if I did well next week in the Championship—"

Mary thought over the plan on her way home and the more she thought about it the better she liked it. There were obviously many advantages in it. The bungalow high up on the hill overlooking the link was quite new and looked fresh and pretty; it could be easily run, far more easily than the old-fashioned type of house. And then the work. How much better it would be to work out of doors all day than to be shut up in a stuffy office!

Mrs. Douglas was against the idea at first—she had other plans for her daughter—but Mary was very persuasive and she was obliged to own that there were points in its favour. Mary was a dear, quite perfect in every way, but she was not very clever at books—

"I wish you need not do anything, Mary," she said for the twentieth time. And Mary replied, also for the twentieth time, "But you see I must do something."

The next day was wet, but rain did not deter Mary; she put on her waterproof and walked over to Greenfell to see the secretary. Mr. Reid had been a friend of her father's, so she had hopes that he might help her. He listened to her request with a smile—the thing was absurd—Mary Douglas a professional at Greenfell! Still, for old time's sake he tried to turn her down kindly.

"You see Mary, we want somebody well known as a sort of advertisement for the club."

Mary saw. "If I were to do well in the Championship?" she suggested.

"If you were to win it, we would take you."

"You promise that?"

"Yes, I promise—but it's not likely, is it?"

"I shall have a good try, Mr. Reid," said Mary gaily.

Mr. Reid stroked his chin,"

"You know that Miss Clutterbuck is coming north for it," he said. "Wonderful player—simply wonderful. Saw her the other day at Deal. Remarkable precision—her iron shots—her approaches—"

"I *will* beat her," said Mary Douglas, clenching her hand and thinking of the little red bungalow on the hill.

2

That evening Mary went to see an old friend of hers, a queer old Italian woman who kept a little curiosity shop full of china and antiques in Port Andrew High Street. The place had fascinated Mary when she was a child and it still lured her. Madame Goiya, as she was called in the village, was not the least attractive antique in the shop. She was an old woman but she had been beautiful in her day and there was something strange and dignified about her now. Her eyes were dark brown, soft and shiny and her olive skin was still smooth.

Mary went in quietly and found Madame Goiya huddled over a fire in the shop.

"It is so cold," she said. "And I am not young as I once was. Sometimes I long for my warm and beautiful home till it hurts me here."

She put a small olive hand on her heart and looked up at Mary with a sad smile.

"Is it impossible for you to go, Madame?" asked Mary sympathetically.

"Not impossible, perhaps, that is a big word, but very difficult for an old woman to go so far alone. You know that my son is dead—he would have taken me … but now tell me about your affairs, Miss Mary."

Nothing loathe, the girl sat down and poured out her troubles and hopes to her old friend. Madame was a good confidante; she listened carefully, nodding her head and putting in an occasional question which showed that she was interested.

"This plan of yours sounds good to me," she said at last. "You are a child of the open air—you simply would not thrive in an office indoors all day working with a pen. We should all work with our best talent and yours is the golf-club, is it not?"

"I'm afraid it is," Mary admitted. "I'm not much use at anything else."

A little silence fell, a friendly peaceful silence. The firelight winked and glittered over a hundred queer objects which made up Madame Goiya's stock-in-trade. The suit of armour which had stood in the corner by the door ever since Mary could remember seemed to come alive; one could imagine a pair of bright eyes shining through the visor of the ancient helmet. The old brass knockers, handles and coalscuttles reflected the red light of the fire from their polished surfaces while the tapestry which hung upon the walls seemed to suck up every ray of light and added to the gloom. Madame herself seemed part of it all; her voice seemed to come from the past with an echo of forgotten glories. She too was an antique wrested from her natural setting, an alien to the twentieth century, strange and beautiful, kindling the imagination.

They talked of many things in that strange room, and when at last Mary rose to go, it was with a sigh of reluctance.

The Italian laughed, well pleased at the compliment.

"I am very old and I have seen a great many things," she said gently. "Come back again soon and we shall have more interesting talk. Come back very soon and you shall have something pretty. I have a box of things coming to me from my beautiful Italy and I will find something in it for you."

"Of course I will come back soon," said Mary quickly. "But I don't need any bribe to come and see you—you know that Madame."

"Who said bribe?" cried the old woman indignantly. "May I not give a little present to my good friend without this talk of bribes?"

3

Port Andrew had seen three days of excellent golf— even the old fogies in the window of the men's clubhouse were bound to admit the fact. Women were no longer content to play an inferior game; these lithe girls drove the ball as far as most men and their short game was a joy to watch.

Miss Clutterbuck sailed through her half of the draw and reached the semi-final with the ease of long experience. She rarely made a mistake (*never* some people said), her tall strongly built figure in its perfectly cut tweed coat and skirt was always the centre of an admiring crowd. She was like a rock, solid and inscrutable; not one of her opponents was able to take her beyond the fifteenth green.

Mary Douglas had several tough matches in her half of the draw but she struggled through somehow—more by good luck than good guidance as she admitted to her friend Dora Inglis. The truth was that Mary was off her game—perhaps the very determination to win interfered with the calm repose of mind so necessary to the game.

The fourth day was the final between the local girl and the champion. It was to be a thirty-six hole match and nobody had much doubt of the result. At the club the odds, when anyone would take them, were about 10 to 1 on the champion. Even Mary herself, indomitable little soul though she was, began to feel hopeless and despondent.

The day of the final was bright and cool with a keen steady breeze from the east. A perfect day for golf! Mary felt her spirits rise as she walked down to the tee.

"Even if I am beaten it will be a good game, but I will win, I will—" she said to herself.

Miss Clutterbuck was waiting at the first tee. She looked large and grim and immaculate; not a crease marred her perfectly hung skirt, not a wrinkle in her well cut coat. She nodded to Mary in a casual manner which without being actually rude showed that she considered it condescension to play at all, and was feeling bored at the prospect. Mary's blood boiled, which was perhaps the best thing that could have happened. She grasped her driver and drove a fine straight ball down the centre of the course. Her opponent followed suit and the two moved off followed by their respective caddies and a tremendous crowd. Every man, woman and child in Port Andrew who could manage it had taken a holiday that day to see the match, for Mary Douglas was a general favourite in the town and they all hoped to see her beat the champion.

Both players approached well, and the first hole was halved in four. The second was halved in three and the third went to Mary by virtue of a long putt. After this, however, Miss Clutterbuck settled down grimly and Mary found herself losing ground. She held on pluckily enough but by the end of the morning's round she was four down.

"It's pretty hopeless," she said to Dora Inglis as the two

walked home to lunch.

"Nonsense," replied Dora, with a confidence she was far from feeling. "The woman has shot her bolt—wait till you have had your lunch—"

They were passing down the High Street when a boy ran out from Madame Goiya's shop.

"Please to come—Madame's wanting tae see you," he said to Mary.

Dora seized her friend's arm. "You've no time. Come and have your lunch," she said urgently.

Mary hesitated for a moment and then, remembering how ill the old poor woman had looked, she decided to go in and see her.

"I shan't stay long," she told Dora.

After the glare of the noonday street the little shop was dim and shadowy. Madame was sitting by the fire wrapped in a crimson dressing gown; she looked smaller than ever, her olive face seemed to have shrunk and become even more foreign and strange.

"It is good of you to come," she said, smiling at Mary. "I have something for you today."

"I hope you are better."

Madame Goiya shook her head so that the big gold earrings winked and twinkled in the firelight.

"It is no matter. Look what I have got for you today."

She held out a little silver trinket in her thin hand with its long tapering fingers.

"Take it, dear Missie. It will bring a wish to you."

Mary took it and looked at it curiously. It was a little silver charm much worn and polished by age so that the lettering on it was unreadable.

"What a queer shape it is!" Mary said.

"Yes—it is a spell," replied Madame in her slow husky voice. "It brings wishes, one to each. It came in the box from Italy and I have put a new ribbon on it for you."

"How do you mean, it brings wishes?" Mary said as she slipped the ribbon over her head.

"It is a spell," Madame repeated with a puzzled wrinkling of her brows. "I cannot tell you more. To each person it brings one wish. I have wished my wish and it is coming to me soon."

"What did you wish?"

"To go away from this place with its so cold winds and rains—but no matter what I wish, an old woman who has had her life—you are young, see, you will wish for love or wealth. But you must tell nobody or the charm will be spoiled. Wear it for the sake of the old woman who has liked you for your kindness."

Mary thanked her for the gift. The charm had something very attractive about it; the queer shape and the polished smoothness betokened great age and constant wear. Who had fashioned it with such care and cunning, who had worn it so consistently?

Mary came out of her little reverie to hear Dora calling her.

"Goodbye, Madame," she said, taking the thin old hand in hers. "I hope your wish will come true for I know you have been unhappy in Port Andrew ever since your son died—but I shall miss you dreadfully if you go away."

"It will come very soon," replied Madame confidently.

4

"You have not left yourself much time for lunch," said Dora reproachfully.

"Madame Goiya is going away and wanted to say goodbye," replied Mary. For some reason she felt she did not want to tell Dora about the charm which was now hanging round her neck inside her jumper. She put up her hand and felt the little hard lump it made against her breast. Of course there was nothing in it really, but it would be rather fun to try—tonight in her room when she was going to bed. What should she wish for? Wealth, perhaps—certainly not love (the modern girl feels no need for that until the right man comes.)

When she walked back to the first tee after a sensible lunch, Mary felt steadied and more able to meet her opponent. "While there's life there's hope," she told herself firmly. "After all the woman is only human, and golf—is golf. Anything may happen, so cheer up, Mary Douglas!"

Her caddy was waiting for her and smiled encouragingly.

"All the caddies are wanting us tae win."

"We'll do our best," replied Mary.

She did her best, and it was very good but it was discouraging work. Miss Clutterbuck started four up and her golf was perfect. There were no flaws in it; she had not a weak stroke in her repertoire. Mary felt as if she were beating up against a brick wall. She held her ground but in spite of all her efforts she could make no advance. At the 27th hole she was still four down—four down and nine to play.

Dora pushed through the crowd to her friend's side.

"Buck up," she whispered. "There's still time. You are playing magnificently—I've never known you play better."

"I know," said Mary. "But I'm not good enough all the same. I wish the woman would make a mistake occasionally."

At the next hole both players got perfect drives; the balls lay within a few yards on each other on the fairway. It was Mary to play the odd. She consulted her caddy for a moment and decided to take her spoon. The ball soared away like a bird and landed on the green. A murmur went up from the crowd for it was a fine shot.

Miss Clutterbuck chose a driving iron and hit the ball with her usual assurance but to Mary's amazement it curled round to the right and disappeared amongst some gorse bushes.

"She sliced it," said Dora incredulously. "Hit it right in the socket—I saw her—"

Miss Clutterbuck herself was evidently surprised; she examined her club critically and handed it back to the caddy with gesture of disgust. It was obvious that she was not used to socketing her iron shots and did not like the experience. The hole went to Mary.

The next hole, a long one, was halved carefully in five. It was good golf and neither player was taking risks. Number thirteen is short and tricky and today it provided plenty of thrills for the audience.

Mary topped her tee shot into a bunker; she was well

out in two but her opponent's ball lay within a club's length of the hole. Mary had to play two more. She looked carefully at her putt, which was a long one, downhill with a puzzling bias, then she hit it squarely. The ball rolled down slowly and trickled into the hole.

"It's no good though," she said to Dora. "Miss Clutterbuck has that putt for it and I've never seen her miss one."

Miss Clutterbuck took her putter and settled down to her stroke but somehow or other she misjudged the distance and failed to hole it. The hole was halved.

"That has rattled her," said a man in the crowd.

It had evidently done so for at the next hole she topped her drive and although she made a good recovery from the rough, the hole went to the local girl.

The excitement was now intense: Mary was only two down. There was not a sound from the crowd as the two players teed up at the fourteenth (which was of course the thirty-second hole of the match).

Both balls got well away and lay together upon the fairway within a hundred yards of the hole. Mary pitched hers over a couple of bunkers onto the green; it ran past the hole for about ten yards. Miss Clutterbuck saw that Mary had over-run the hole and evidently decided to spare hers. She misjudged the distance by about a foot and rolled back into a deep bunker.

"Hard luck!" said Mary impulsively.

Miss Clutterbuck glared at her.

"Bad play," she snapped and signed to her caddy to pick up the ball.

94

Mary's heart gave a little flutter of excitement as she led the way to the next tee. She was keyed up to concert pitch, every nerve strung. Outwardly however she was perfectly calm and collected.

The last three holes fell to Mary without much trouble; Miss Clutterbuck's game seemed to be completely disorganised by her mistakes. All the zip had gone out of her iron shots and she was timid on the greens. She took her defeat badly and openly showed her resentment and disgust. Mary could not help feeling sorry for her and this feeling dimmed her pleasure of her victory.

"What on earth happened to her?" Dora whispered.

Everyone in the crowd was asking the same thing.

"Och well!" said Mary's caddy. "Ye see yon wumman's no accustomed to makin' mistakes an' the thing jis gripped her."

The match finished on the thirty-sixth green where a huge crowd had gathered to watch the last hole. When Mary's victory was announced there was a great cheer, for everyone was delighted at the result. To do Port Andrew justice, it would have cheered for Miss Clutterbuck too, for we are nothing if not sporting. All Mary's friends gathered round her and told her how well she had played and shook her hand till it was quite sore.

"But she's ever so much better than I am," Mary kept saying. "Only somehow she went to pieces—"

5

It was late and getting dark when at last Mary tore herself away from her friends and walked slowly home.

She felt very tired after the excitement but she was happy for she knew that Mr. Reid would keep his promise and that the post she coveted was hers. She and her mother would move into that dear little house and their troubles would be at an end. Life was good. She stopped at the door of Madame Goiya's shop and peeped in—it would be nice to tell her old friend of her success—

"Is Madame in?" she said to the small boy who had started to put up the shutters.

He looked up at her with tear-reddened eyes.

"She's gone."

"Gone!" echoed Mary. "But I saw her this morning—where has she gone?"

"She's deid," he sobbed incoherently. "An' I dinna want her to be deid. She was aye guid to me—an' noo she's deid."

Mary steadied herself against the lintel of the door. So that was where she had gone—'away from the cold winds and the rains.' Her wish had come soon.

The small charm dangled from Mary's neck; she put up her hand and felt it beneath her jumper, and suddenly a thought flashed through her mind and she caught her breath.

"So I've had my wish too," she said, and smiled involuntarily at the queer thought. Was Miss Clutterbuck beaten by black magic? Or was it merely a coincidence? To this day Mary Douglas is not quite sure—

MISTRESS
MACNABBERTY

MISTRESS MACNABBERTY

"THERE IS NO DOUBT about it, poverty has its advantages as well as its disadvantages," proclaimed a loud strident voice from our home-made wireless set. Alec stretched out a hand and turned it off. "We don't want to listen to that rubbish," he said, a trifle bitterly. Personally I wouldn't have minded hearing it, I wouldn't have minded hearing the man's views on the advantages of poverty. The disadvantages are apparent, of course.

"The man's probably rolling in money himself," said Alec, "or he would not think there was any advantage at all in being poor."

I was bound to agree that there was some truth in the statement; personally I have only discovered one advantage in being poor and that a temporary, dirty, careless, noisy, cheerful person who calls herself and insists on being called Mistress Macnabberty.

Alec says I must be crazy to put Mistress Macnabberty on the credit side because only last week, I declared, almost with tears, that the woman was driving me mad. But somehow or other, even when I think of all the amazing and unexpected things that Mistress Macnabberty does and continues gaily to do even after I have pointed out to her the hygienic principles which she is violating by so doing, I feel it would be dull to return to the machine-like ministrations of Lily and Bella who ordered our lives for us until the necessity for strict economy made their dismissal imperative.

Since the advent of Mistress Macnabberty the tempo of life has gone faster. She fills the kitchen premises with her high falsetto voice; her repertoire is limited to "Oh God of Bethel" and a selection of ancient music hall ditties of questionable propriety. She invests the most ordinary household duties with an aura of excitement and danger.

"I never turn back a bed," said Mistress Macnabberty, as together we turned back the bed. "I never turn back a bed but I think mebbe there's a snake lying beneath the claes all currled up like a spring ready tae leap at me."

And yet this amazing woman had never seen a snake, "no a reel live yin, ye ken", not even in the Zoo.

"What wud the likes o' me be daein' at the Zoo? Jis' wastin' a saxpence that's a'. Snakes!" said Mistress Macnabberty scornfully. "There's nae need tae gang tae the Zoo tae see snakes. I'm not wantin' tae see snakes efter yon time I had wi' Jeames. Jeames saw snakes an' geeraffes an' puggies tae—'Och Maggie,' he wud shriek. 'They're hinging doon fra' the roof by their tails.' Losh it wus fair awfi'! An' I'm tellin' ye, Mistress Broon, efter a wee while I wus seein' them masel'. Na, na, keep yer saxpence—it's no that I'm ungratefu' either, ye ken."

Mistress Macnabberty is short and broad so that her silhouette on the kitchen wall as she reaches for a plate off the dresser is perfectly square. Her forearm is like a ham and with it she scours the kitchen table until it is white as driven snow (but alas, she leaves dark corners severely alone.) Her face is square also, and of a peculiar bright pink colour which tones ill with the bright red hair in which it is framed. This bright red hair of hers spends most of its time screwed so tightly into curl papers that her small eyes are dragged up at the corners till she looks for all the world like a pink variety of chinese mandarin. She has a wide mouth and several gaps in her teeth which show to disadvantage when she smiles.

"That wus Jeames," she says cheerfully when I sympathise with her upon their loss. "I never wus at a dentist in ma life. Jeames went for me wit the fire-tongs an' I wus lucky tae escape wi' ma life, for the puir soul was dementit. Yon wus his last eellness, ye ken, Mistress Broon, an' he never rose fra' his bed again. Losh me, I lost a guid man when Jeames deed! Ugha, I did that."

I got to know James quite well as the days went by and Mistress Macnabberty, who had come to "help tempory" stayed on and continued to make us uncomfortable; few details of his last illness were hidden from me as we worked the house together.

"I never open the oven door tae luik at a cake," Mistress Macnabberty announced one day, suiting the action to the words, "but I think on Mistress Whinney. The Whinneys lived next door yon time we were in Stairling, an' she wus a Great One for ee-conomy. 'Gyptian eggs wus all the go, yon time, an' Mistress Whinney put a few in the oven tae bake for their suppers, an' when Mester Whinney opened the oven door the heat had hatched them oot, an' there wus a wheen wee lezzards rinning aboot the oven—"

"Not really!" I exclaimed, aghast.

"Weel, I didna' see them masel," Mistress Macnabberty

allowed, with true Scottish caution. "It wus Mester Whinney tellt me—an' he wasna' that keen on 'gyptian eggs. Whiles I've wunnered ef mebbe he didna' mek up the hale thing tae pit his wife aff buying them."

Mistress Macnabberty has a strange habit of serving our food on the nearest dish that she can lay her hands on. Alec and I have got quite used to seeing our potatoes appear on a large soup plate covered with the lid of the soup tureen, and the baked apples in the vegetable dish. Sometimes the breakfast eggs and bacon come to table in a soufflé dish and sometimes on a kitchen plate with an upturned pudding bowl over it to keep it hot. I have spoken to her about it several times, and she always listens carefully with her kindly smile and promises to remember, but she never does.

"I get a wee thing flustered, ye ken," she admits sadly, "an I'm that keen for ye tae get the things while they're hot, I jis' tak' the nearest dish an' never think what I'm daein'."

Who could be angry with the woman? After all she is quite a good cook in a plain unimaginative way and the things taste just as good; but the day that Alec's mother was coming to lunch I thought it wiser to lay out the suitable dishes before going up to dress.

"Pit the dishes in their right order, Mistress Broon," said Mistress Macnabberty, lifting a hot, pink face from basting the fowl. "I'm no wantin' tae affront ye wi' yon wumman here."

I put the dishes in their right order on the dresser, first the soup-tureen, and then the deep glass fireproof dish for

102

the fowl, and then the ashet for the steamed pudding. How could I have foreseen that the strange creature would serve the fowl before the soup, and serve it faithfully in the first dish which she found upon the dresser. My heart sank when the fowl arrived at table in the soup-tureen, and sank still further when the soup followed after, swimming about most dangerously in the glass dish. I forgave her that of course, (it was partly my own fault for not telling her in what order we wished to eat our meal) but it was harder to forgive her for serving the sauce for the pudding in the kitchen milk-jug which unfortunately had been bereft of its handle. Alec's mother was not the sort of person to permit even kitchen milk-jugs to lack handles.

All this was bad enough, and Alec was well within his rights when he besought me to dismiss the woman and get somebody with a little more savoir faire. I knew that I ought to dismiss the woman but I simply couldn't do it. Mistress Macnabberty had won my heart, she was so amusing, she was so human, she didn't mind how much work she did. Alec saw my point. "Well, keep her then," he said, "but don't blame me—"

I didn't blame him; I didn't blame anybody but myself for the awful thing that happened last week at my tea party. Perhaps it was rash to attempt a tea party with Mistress Macnabberty in the house, but I had got used to her by this time and of course I could manage the tea by myself. There was no need for Mistress Macnabberty to appear upon the scenes at all, and my guests need never know that such a person existed. Mistress Macnabberty was washing that afternoon, and attired as she always was on washing-days in an old red flannel skirt and a bright green cardigan pinned across her ample breast with a large safety pin. She was a grand washer, in fact my only difficulty on washing days was to keep her from washing everything in the house that she could lay her hands on. Her washing on that particular day was larger than usual; it occupied her whole attention, the back green was festooned with garments of every shape and hue. It happened to be a hard frost, and I sprinkled the front door steps with salt in the time-honoured manner so that there should be no chance of my guests breaking their legs.

Tea went off well, Mistress Macnabberty's scones were enjoyed and admired: she made excellent scones. We were talking about the latest books, and Mrs. McDermid was laying down the law about the dreadful strain of vulgarity in Modern Literature when the drawing room door burst open and Mistress Macnabberty appeared. She was hot and flushed and triumphant, and her arms up to the elbow were clean and pink with their immersion in hot soap suds. In one hand she held the trousers, and in the other hand the jacket of a pair of Alec's oldest and shabbiest pyjamas. The garments had been frozen stiff with the unusually severe frost—the legs were like boards, the coat frozen into a weird shape with arms outstretched.

"Luik at yon!" exclaimed Mistress Macnabberty in the dead silence which followed her entrance. "Is that no comic, Mistress Broon? I couldna rest till I'd brocht them in tae show you an' yer freends. Did ye ever see the like, for I never did?"

She danced the legs about on the carpet to amuse my guests and then overcome by the humour of it she threw back her head and laughed and laughed.

It was this episode which almost reduced me to tears and gave rise to my remark that the woman was driving me mad. That was last week, and I am still wondering whether I should get rid of Mistress Macnabberty and look for somebody more conventional in her behaviour— or not.

WINTERING
A narrative in blank verse

WINTERING

THE HOSPITAL

"I hope you wintered well," said old Miss Brown.
"It was Sardinia last year, was it not?
Before that, Costa Brava. People say
The Austrian Alps have now become the rage
But p'raps this year you spread your wings and flew
To far New Zealand, where the Maoris bathe
In boiling water from volcanic springs?
I am too old to venture far afield
I sit at home and read," said old Miss Brown.

I smiled and said I had been "far afield"
And this was true. So far afield I'd been
From usual haunts of fashionable friends
I'd given up the struggle to come back.
Here in this quiet ward, this nun-like cell
Within the busy hospital I'd close
My eyes for evermore and say good-bye
To all the joys and sorrows of the world.

But this was not to be, for gentle hands
Had soothed my fretfulness and blessed drugs
Had brought me ease from pain. Then, day by day;
The mists receded and my strength returned.

At last one morning when the doctor came
He smiled and said, "You're getting better now:
The deadly virus is in full retreat.
We've done our bit, it's up to you to climb
The hill to health — a hard and stony hill!
Goodbye, Miss Dale. Take my advice, be wise
Fly out to Tripoli or Tenerife.
There you will find bright sunshine and blue skies."

A feeble ghost it was that tottered forth,
Forth from the warmth and comfort of the ward;
A fragile thing that scarce had strength to walk,
A creature that could neither eat nor sleep
And trembled at an unexpected sound.
For weeks the doctors' will had been my law;
I'd drunk his potions, swallowed coloured pills
And suffered sharp injection at his 'hest . . .
But Tripoli? No, no, nor Tenerife,
Nor any foreign shore! How could I fly
In this strange weakened state? Where could I go?
'Twas peace I needed. Where could I find peace?
Not in this busy town, this noisy world,
This world of bustling men and hooting cars,
Three days of horrid torture I endured
Shut up inside my flat, afraid to move.

MRS. MAPP

"They've let you out too soon," said Mrs. Mapp,
Who came and cleaned the flat three times a week.

"That doctor should have had more sense — but there,
Perhaps he wants the bed for someone else!
You're in a nice old mess — that's what I think.
You'll get no better sitting by the fire
All by yourself, and thinking of your woes.
You mustn't fret about your pictures, dear."

My "pictures" (as she called them) were indeed
A source of worry to my anxious mind.
I had a contract with a publisher
To illustrate his books. I had designed
Attractive jackets for his paperbacks
Pictures for little children's story-books
Or comic skits for women's magazines.
I had a Seeing Eye, a cunning hand,
I found good copy everywhere I went,
And that surprisingly, was how I earned
My daily bread . . .
                    But I had lost the art.
My pencil, once so busy, idle now,
My one small talent dead . . .

"I liked your pictures," added Mrs. Mapp
In sympathetic tones. "They made me smile
And p'raps some day when you are strong and fit
You'll draw some more . . .
                    You need a change of air . . ."
I shook my head and sadly I replied:
"I need a deep dark hole in which to hide."
"What about that?" the kindly woman asked,

And with a stubby finger pointed out
The modest little advert, in *The Times:*
"A clergyman and wife would take a guest
For several months at reasonable charge
To share their quiet home at Wick-on-Sea."

"Write now," said Mrs. Mapp persuasively.
"It wouldn't be my cup of tea, of course
But you could try it, couldn't you, my dear?
You'll never get any better staying here."

I knew that she was right. I seized my pen.
I wrote in haste, for I was desperate.
I said I had been ill . . . wanted a change
And peace and quiet to restore my health.
I said "Please phone at once if I may come."
The letter, badly written, ill expressed,
Should have been copied out in neater form
But Mrs. Mapp was waiting to go home
And so I let her take it to the post.

No sooner had she gone than I was filled
With vain regrets for my impulsive deed,
And waited anxiously for the result.

THE OPEN DOOR

I had not long to wait: "Is that Miss Dale?"
Asked Mrs. Trevor in a gentle voice.

"We're very sorry you have been so ill.
The room is rather small. It faces west
So you will get the evening sun of course.
And we shall do our best to care for you
And make you comfortable in our house."

Dear fools — dear holy innocents they were!
They asked no references. I might have been
A criminal for all they knew — or cared.
Their door was open to me, open wide!

"How good of you!" I said in trembling tones.
"Oh, not at all! You'll come by train of course?
Edward will meet you with our little car
On Saturday at ten minutes to four."

TEA IN THE PARLOUR

Tea in the parlour at the Vicarage:
A peaceful haven far from madding crowds;
A faded carpet, pictures on the walls,
Old-fashioned furniture and easy chairs.
The tea-table, drawn up beside the fire,
Was covered with a white embroidered cloth
And on it was an ancient silver tray
A plate of little cakes and toasted buns.

"Oh, you are young, Miss Dale!" my hostess cried.
"We thought you would be old — or elderly.

Come and sit down. You must be very cold
After your tiresome journey in the train."
The vicar smiled and said he, too, had been
Surprised to find "the aged guest" was young.
Poker in hand he coaxed the little fire
Into a cheerful blaze. Then tea was brought
In silver pot of goodly size and shape.
They were so kind — already I felt soothed
And warmed and comforted. There was no need
For me to talk . . . I listened and relaxed.

WINTER IS BEST

"Ah, this is what I like," the vicar said.
"Tea and a toasted bun beside the fire
Is twice as pleasant as a 'garden tea'
With lettuce and tomato sandwiches . . .
And wasps in black and yellow pullovers
Buzzing around the elderberry jam."

He paused, then added with a beaming smile,
"There is a welcome freshness in the air
Which heralds winter days and winter ways.
The caravans in Higginbotham's field
Are being towed away and Mrs. Leake
Has shut her "Gifte Shoppe" in the village street."

"We like the winter best," his wife explained.
"In winter Wick-on-Sea is all our own.

D. E. Stevenson, aged 3

With younger sister Kathleen

D. E. Stevenson's wedding portrait, 1916

With her husband, Major James R. Peploe

With Annie Patricia Reid Peploe "Patsy" (1916 -1928)

A picnic with her husband

Family Group: Robin, Rosemary and John
Dorothy and James Peploe

At Dryburgh Abbey with daughter Rosemary

Playing tennis with elder son Robin

"I write all my books in longhand, lying on a sofa near the window in my drawing room." With son Robin

The villagers revert to peaceful ploys:
Fishing and mending nets, tilling the ground
Is better, far, than selling 'Souvenirs'
(Rubbish from foreign lands) to visitors
At twice the proper price. Edward has tried
Without avail to stop the sinful trade."

The Vicar, taking up the thread, went on:
"Winter is best. The big hotel is closed,
The villagers take down their notices
Offering Bed and Breakfast for a song.
The buses cease to clutter up the roads
And belch their noxious fumes. The ice-cream man
(A handsome fellow with a lustful eye)
Vanishes to an unknown habitat.
In winter I can walk along the shore
Without the pain of seeing rows of legs
And naked bodies blist'ring in the sun;
Without the pain of seeing tender babes
Imbibing brightly-coloured fizzy drinks
Thus ruining the linings of their tums."

I had to laugh.
                 "Edward! Miss Dale will think
We do not love our neighbours as we should!"
Said Mrs. Trevor with a rueful smile.

"It is because we love them, Mary dear,"
'Edward' explained. "Alas, I know full well
The dire effects of sunburn on a skin

Exposed too suddenly to violet rays!
I am a kindly man, therefore I grieve
For all the misery they'll have to bear
During the silent watches of the night."

CECILIA'S STORY

The little cakes and buns were finished now
But still we did not move. The talk flowed on:
And now my tongue was loosened and I found
That I could speak to them about myself.
I felt that they had every right to know
The circumstances of their stranger-guest.

I told them something of my lonely state:
Father and mother dead — no relatives.
Oh, I had friends of course — a host of friends!
Friends for fair weather, none for rainy days.
Not one (not even Agnes Thistlewood,
Whom I'd accounted "best") had spared the time
To come and see me in the hospital.

Then in return for this — this dismal tale —
I was awarded gentle sympathy:
Murmurs of sweet compassion for my plight.

At last the vicar sighed and said, "Miss Dale,
Mary and I are honoured that you feel
Sufficiently at home with us to speak

Thus frankly of your sad and troubled life.
Our life has been a smooth and easy path:
Last week we had our Silver Wedding Day —
Twenty five years of close companionship
Has been our lot (no cloud has marred our bliss).
Therefore we sat and wondered how to show
Our gratitude in word — and deed — to God."

He stopped and looked at Mary. "Yes," said she.

MARY'S IDEA

"Mary's idea, it was," the Vicar said.
"Mary suggested we should take a guest:
A frail old lady, lonely, silver-haired,
And make her welcome in our hearts and home.
Hence the advertisement in Tuesday's *Times.*"

"Was mine the only answer you received?"

"Oh no," was the reply. "We'd had half a score
The letters fluttered in by every post.
One of the ladies sent a reference
Which said she was an angel in the house."

"Too good for us," said Mary with a smile.
"Too good," Edward agreed in solemn tones.
"It would have been an awful strain for us
Trying to live up to such a guest."

117

"Others there were who wanted this — or that.
Miss Green wants golf — her handicap is Scratch.
Miss Trump delights in Bridge; Miss Jones in Squash
And Mrs. Sponge must have a private bath.

"Miss Manx has got a precious pussikins
Who's going to have a lot of kittikins
And therefore must be fed on fish and cream.
Miss Sprout, a vegetarian for years,
Enclosed a comprehensive diet sheet;
The Lady Ermyntrude of Wester Spar
Desired a heated garage for her car.

"Who else? Oh, Mrs. Lily Smythe of course!
She sent a letter from her Parish Priest
Who praised her interest in Church Affairs
And, what is more, he's sure that we shall find
Refreshment in her keen and well-stocked mind."

The Vicar paused to laugh . . .
                              "Then why?" I cried,
"Why choose Cecilia Dale to be your guest?"

The answer, simple as at first it seemed,
Disclosed the wealth of kindness in their hearts
And understanding of humanity
As true and deep and wise as Solomon's.

"She asked no questions, craved no benefits
We thought her need was greatest," Mary said.

Sadly I murmured, "But it is not too late
To change our plan. I must find somewhere else —
Some other place where I can rest awhile — "

The Vicar interrupted with a smile.

"Miss Dale shall guide our choice. That's only fair.
Miss Green wants golf. Perhaps a putting course
Upon the lawn would test her wondrous skill.
Or must we allocate our only bath
To the fastidious Mrs. Percy Sponge?
Or shall we teach our Hilda to prepare
Nut cutlets and raw carrots for Miss Sprout?
Or must we build — no matter what the cost—
A garage for my Lady's Jaguar?
Say not that we must learn to entertain
Miss Bridget Trump . . ."

                              "No, no!" I cried
"It must be Mrs. Smythe, that's very clear.
The lady with the keen and well-stocked mind
Who takes an interest in Church Affairs,
She would be very useful to you in your work."

The Vicar disagreed. Sadly he said,
"I'd almost rather have Miss Pussikins."

"Edward is teasing you. We've made our choice,"
Said Mary Trevor in her quiet voice.

THE FRUGAL MEAL

Our supper was at eight: (grilled sole, it was,
Honey and bread and butter, coffee, milk),
Then once again, we sat beside the fire
In peace and comfort. All was settled now,
So Mary told me how she ran the house
And carried out her social work as well:

Hilda was Edward's god-child, aged sixteen,
Who daily came upon her bicycle
To wash and clean and learn domestic work.
"I could not do without her," Mary said.
"Dear Hilda learns so quickly, tries so hard.
Some day, when she is older, she will make
A splendid wife . . . but there is time for that.
Hilda is just a sweetly-natured child
Innocent as the saint whose name she bears."

THE HORNED HATS

"Not so," the Vicar said. "No saint, this maid!
There's pagan blood in Hilda's ancestry.
Listen and you shall hear the reason why
The girl is tall and strong and passing brave,
With golden hair and eyes like summer's sky.

"In days gone by the Long Boats havened here
And Viking from the North brought wild alarms

To all the country-side. Huge men they were,
Ruthless as desert lions. Fire, murder, rape,
Was their delight. Gold hats with horns they wore
Upon their yellow hair — a fearsome sight!
The people fled before their swift advance
And hid in caves or in the darksome woods
And wept to see their simple little homes
Laid waste by fire and smoke and cruel hands.

"The raiders brought destruction far and wide
And then, retreating to their wooden boats,
They rowed away to ravage other lands.
But some there where who, wounded in the fray
Or tired of wandering, remained behind;
Built house and home, took wives, raised families,
Hunted the hills and tilled the fallow ground.
('Wic'k was a village in their Mother-tongue,
'Beck' was a mountain stream and 'fell' a hill)
So, for a time, they were content to dwell
In their adopted land.

                Then came a day!
A fine Spring morning with a spanking breeze
Stirred up strange longings in their pagan hearts . . .
The Sea, their mistress, called them to her arms;
Called them to High Adventure . . .

                     There's the tale,"
Said Edward Trevor with his boyish smile.
"Some of it's true (the Vikings left their mark

Upon this land of ours) and some of it
Is Edward's story for an autumn night
To entertain a guest and to explain
Why English Hilda is so large and fair."

AND SO TO BED

My room was "rather small" but fresh and bright
With every comfort that a guest could wish.
Below the window lay a garden plot
With flow'rs and verdant lawn and winding path.
Beyond, a hill rose steeply to a ridge
Where stood a little church embowered in trees:
Beeches and oaks and spreading sycamores.

The moon, new-risen in a cloudless sky,
Threw coal-black velvet shadows on the grass
And, drifting through my window, came the scent
Of sweetly fragrant white tobacco flowers . . .
And far off murmurs from the restless sea.

"Have you all you want?" my hostess asked.
"You must be tired, perhaps we talked too long?
We are so glad you've come to us, my dear.
We'd like to call you by your Christian name:
It's such a lovely name — and suits you well.
I hope you will be happy here —"

                                        "Oh yes!
I shall be happy in this peaceful place

With you and Edward both so good and kind."
"But we are old," said Mary with a sigh.
"Perhaps you'll find it dull with us, my child?"

To me, despite their years and silver hair
They seemed quite young: innocent children, both.
Mary was saintly. Peace was in her face,
And love and joy and goodness — all the fruits
For which sad mortals strive and strive in vain!
Edward was merry, full of little jokes
(Sometimes a little naughty, Mary thought).
She loved him as a mother loves her child.

We said "Goodnight" and then I went to sleep
And slept . . . and slept . . . and slept without a dream.

HILDA'S STORY

"Breakfast in bed," my hostess had decreed.
'Twas Hilda came to bring the laden tray
And bashfully she said, "The mistress hopes
You rested peacefully — and so do I.
They've gone to church of course but will be home
Soon after nine."

          Then with an anxious frown,
"Have I remembered everything, Miss Dale?
A pot of tea; a glass of orange juice;
A brown egg, lightly boiled; a jug of milk;
Sugar and salt, a roll and marmalade . . ."

123

"Yes, you've remembered everything," I said
And thanked her for her care.

                        "The roll was made
Early this morning in my father's shop.
He is the baker here, at Wick-on-Sea
Especially for you he gave it me
And bade me bring it with me when I came."
"For me? How did he know — ?"

                              She laughed and said,
"Everyone knows that Miss Cecilia Dale
Had come to convalesce at Wick-on-Sea.
Everyone hopes that she will soon be well."
Oh, she was good and kind, this woman-child,
And tall and straight. Sweet as a summer morn.
Her plaited hair was wound about her head —
A coronet as bright as August corn!

And then, with some encouragement from me,
Hilda began to tell me of her home:
A little cottage in the village street
With modern shop and bakery close by.
Two hundred years the business had come down —
Father to son, without a single break!
Her father, Robert Hood, was sixth in line
To bake the daily bread for Wick-on-Sea.

At first it was a small concern, but now
Owing to Robert's energy and skill
His business was expanding, week by week.
He had rebuilt his property

And brought it up to date in modern style
With all the latest gadgets for his trade.
He had engaged two lads and trained them well
To mix the dough and bake the little cakes
And crusty loaves of goodly shape and size.
Three vans he'd bought to tour the neighbourhood
With bread and rolls and appetising pies.

Hilda had brothers: Sam, aged seventeen,
And little Peter who was still at school.
"Will they be bakers too?" I asked the girl
For I was interested in her tale.
"Not Sam," said Hilda. "Sam has other plans
He craves Adventure, wants to see the World,
A sailor's life is what our Sam desires.
A famous Admiral was Samuel Hood.
Sam learnt about him when he was at school,
And, ever since, the admiral has been
The hero of our Samuel's wildest dreams:
All that he most admires.
                                    But brother Pete
Is made of diff'rent stuff. He'll be content
To mix the dough and bake the crusty loaves
And fill the pies. Already little Pete
Although so young, is useful in the shop."

She paused. Then, smiling happily, she said
"He'll be the seventh Hood to bake the bread
For Wick-on-Sea . . ."

NEW NEIGHBOURS

Sunday was Edward Trevor's busy day
And Mary's too, of course . . . but after tea
We sat together by the parlour fire.
'Twas then I heard about the village folk
Who were to be my neighbours for a while.

I heard about the Bodgers' clever son:
A garden boy to Colonel Hammerton
Until the Colonel, mindful of his skill
In raising healthy plants and tending flow'rs,
Arranged for Ted to find a post at Kew
And gain a wider knowledge of his trade.
"Tom Bodger will do well," the Vicar said.

"Meanwhile," this Mary Trevor with a sigh,
"Meanwhile the garden at the Hammertons,
Which used to be a joy, has now become
A wilderness in which the Colonel toils
Beyond his strength."

             And then the Trevors spoke
Of Lady Dunscombe at the Manor House:
For years she'd lived a fashionable life,
Had been a leader in Society.
She was a lovely woman, well endowed
With gracious manners and a lively wit
So she had friends galore, both young and old.

But now she had grown tired of junketing,
Tired of the noise and bustle of the town
And had returned to Wick (her childhood home)
To end her days in peaceful solitude.

With her had come some members of her staff:
Faithful retainers, who had served her well
For many years — and now, though old and grey,
Were strong enough to run the Manor House
And serve their lady in her quiet life.

Sometimes the lady had a guest to stay
(One of her many friends who needed rest)
But mostly Lady Dunscombe was alone.

"Alone but never lonely," Mary said.
"She is a painter, famed throughout the world.
Delightful flower-paintings are her line,
She picks the subjects in her flower-beds
Arranges them in diff'rent coloured jars
And paints them in her little studio.
Someday when you are feeling strong enough
I'll take you to the Manor House to call
And you shall see the pictures for yourself."

THE VARLEY BOYS.

The Vicar, taking up the tale, declared
That I must surely meet the Varley twins:

"Like as two peas, grown in the self-same pod"
Edward averred . . . and Mary said so too.

They were away just now but would return
Ere Christmas to their home at Wick-on-Sea.
These lads bred ponies, kept a riding school
At Elderberry Farm. They did not make
A fortune by their work, but none the less
They were a happy pair and full of vim.
Always together, never seen apart,
And rarely seen without their bulldog bitch
Trotting behind their heels. They called her Vi.
'Twas she — and she alone — knew which was which.

THE SERPENT

So then I smiled, and, teasingly, I said
"I've heard about the Hoods and Lady D.
I've heard about the Bodgers' clever son
And now you tell me of the Varley boys —
All happy people, good and kind and wise!
Are there no snakes in lucky Wick-on-Sea,
No serpents in your Eden, may I ask?"

"Well, yes, there's Mrs. Leake," my host replied.
"If I could take the portly Mrs. Leake
And sink her at the bottom of the sea
Our little Wick would be Eden, indeed!
She smiles benignantly, and all the while

Her tongue drips poison into willing ears.
'Oh, one may smile and be a villain';
                                        This the Bard!
His sayings true today as yesterday."

"Oh, Edward, no!" cried Mary, ever quick
To find excuses for her neighbours sins.
"Poor Mrs. Leake! — a trifle warped, maybe!
A little too inquisitive, perhaps,
But kind at heart. Last year at Eastertide
When I was ill she came and asked for me
And brought me flowers. Have you forgotten this?"

"Oh no, dear Mary, I remember well:
Sprays of pink currant with a horrid smell.
Hilda removed the bouquet while you slept —
I helped to burn it in the boiler fire."

So much for Mrs. Leake! I had to laugh —
And even Mary was obliged to smile.

THE THUNDER CLOUD

I was so happy here — the days sped past.
Only one cloud was in my sun-filled sky . . .
True it was still a distant thunder-cloud!
It hovered far away above the hills
Yet sometimes troubled me and broke my rest.
I had some money safely in the Bank —

Enough to see me through the winter months —
But then — what then? I'd have to find some work
Quite diff'rent work from what I'd done before.
My health was better. Still I'd not regained
My Seeing Eye, the Cunning of my hand.
I forced myself to work. I tried and tried . . .
All that I did was lifeless, humourless.
My sketches were unsaleable, I knew.
I tore them up and put them in the fire!

I'd have to find a post where I could earn
Sufficient money for my daily bread —
Perhaps as cook or as a companion-help
To some old lady, needing friendly care.
Perhaps a dressmaker's establishment
Would have a vacancy which I could fill . . .

I did not tell the Trevors of my fears.
Nor ask them for their help and sympathy.
But I would have to tell them ere I left
The temporary shelter of their home.

I'd have to ask them for a reference
To say that I was pleasant in the house,
To say I did not drink nor lie nor steal
And had no other very heinous fault.
What else was there to say? They knew no more
Except what I told them of myself.

THE COLONEL'S HAT

Now that I was better it became a joy
To help my hostess in her daily tasks:
To lay the luncheon table for our meal,
To dust the rooms or to arrange the flowers,
To take a shopping basket on my arm
And sally forth into the village street,
To buy the bread, the fish, the groceries,
And all that was required for household use,
And learn to know my neighbours —
                              All were kind
And most of them enjoyed a friendly chat.

One day when I was in the butcher's shop
I met a man who greeted me with warmth,
As if I were a friend he'd known for life!
Called me by name, hoped I was better now,
Asked for "the Padre and his lady wife" . . .
He was a military man — no doubt of that!

The man was tall and lean, straight as a die,
With weatherbeaten face and silver hair
He wore a suit, well-cut, but old and worn
And, on his head, a most unusual hat.

"I see you're looking at my hat," he said.
"I got it years ago in Inverness,
Wore it for fishing, shooting on the moors,
Wore it for sailing on the Norfolk Broads . . .

This hat's a 'deerstalker' like Sherlock Holmes'
You've seen it in his pictures, I expect?"
I said I liked his hat, it suited him.
(It was unusual — yes — but so was he!)

"Good!" he exclaimed. "I'm very glad of that!
My wife is not so fond of it of course.
She says it is 'a positive disgrace'.
She'd like to make me purchase something new,
But this I steadfastly refuse to do.
I'll tell you why, Miss Dale: this is a hat
Which suits all weathers, shades the eyes from glare
And keeps the rain from trickling down one's spine.
In wintry winds I'm comfortably warm —
I tie the ear-flaps underneath my chin.
In fact my 'deerstalker's' a valued friend
No other headgear could be half as fine."

With that he smiled and bowed and said "Good day,
We'll see you soon for lunch or tea, I hope."

"That's Colonel Hammerton," the butcher said.
"He often does the shopping for his wife.
We like to see him walking down the street
He has a pleasant word for everyone."

"The children love him," added Mr. Bouse.
"They like his smile, they like his little jokes,
They chatter to him like a flock of birds.
Sometimes he buys a bag of toffee-drops

Which he distributes open-handedly.
I've heard him shout, 'Who wants a toffee-drop?'
And then they run and follow him about.

"I've seen him sitting on the wooden seat
Beside the fountain on the village green
With a half of score children clustered round
Listening to the tales he has to tell . . .
Stories about his past in foreign lands!
Stories of Indian days and Indian ways!
He's hunted tigers in the Indian woods
And ridden elephants. . .
                    Our children say
The Colonel's tales are 'better than a book'."

"You've children of your own?"
                        "We've three, Miss Dale.
Jack is eleven, doing well at school,
Rosie is nine and little Bobbie five."

When Mary Trevor heard my tale, she said,
"Oh yes, the Colonel is a perfect dear —
No one so popular in Wick-on-Sea!
He takes an interest in every child.
He's always ready with his good advice
And money too, which he can ill afford,
To start the boys in suitable careers.
The Hammertons had one beloved son
Who died in India many years ago
And ever since the Colonel likes to play

With little girls and boys . . .

                              It's just his way
Of comforting himself for what he lost.
But Mrs. Hammerton is not so wise;
When little Philip died she turned aside
And locked her broken heart against the world."

MISCHIEF MAKERS

I'd made my judgement of the Trevors' work
When first I came to Wick. I loved them both.
And now I loved them better every day.
No people I had met in all the world
Were half as good or half as wise as they.
But now I found that other folk in Wick
Had somewhat diff'rent views about the pair.

For instance stalwart Mrs. Hammerton
Thought Mary Trevor foolish — she was not.
Mary was gentle: she was terrified
Of people with rough manners — that was all!

And others thought that Edward was too gay.
"Not staid enough to be a proper priest,"
I'd heard this whispered in the village street.
'Twas Mrs. Leake who started it, of course,
And Mrs. Smart, her bosom friend agreed.
And Mrs. Ingoldsby looked down her Roman nose
When Edward cracked his harmless little jokes.

Oh well, it didn't matter very much:
These three were mischief-makers in the place
And heartily disliked by one and all,
And Edward Trevor had a host of friends,
Friends who would die for him — if need arose.
They knew his worth — knew he was friend indeed
To those in trouble — knew he was kind and wise,
A rock of strength amongst the shifting sands.
It's true that Edward liked a little fun,
He liked to stir our hearts and make us smile . . .
Why should a Christian wear a gloomy face?

THE TOWER OF BABEL

"The Tower of Babel was a sad affair,"
Edward remarked one night at supper-time.
"If we could understand each other's tongue
And speak it fluently perhaps there'd be
Fewer misunderstandings in the world.

"This thought has come to me because today
Two Danish Ministers of God were here,
I found them looking round St. Matthew's Church.
They longed to hear about the sacred fane.
I longed to slake their curiosity.
St. Matthew's has a stormy history
Which would have interested them, I knew.
They had a little English — not enough!
I had no clue whatever to their tongue,

So we were stumped. It was unfortunate.
I liked their looks and they seemed drawn to me.
A little chat would have been very nice,
But it was not to be.
                              We bowed and smiled
And they then said 'Gott bless' and off they went.

"I watched them go away with deep regret
And then they stopped — and turned — and waved their
                                              hands
And doffed their hats — and bowed and smiled again.
I did the same of course. It must have been
A funny sight to all the passers by.
The Tower of Babel was a sad affair,"
Repeated Edward with a heavy sigh.

"My father said the story was a myth,"
Objected Mary in a doubtful voice.

"Your father was a very able man —
I should not care to disagree with him —
And there are many clever gentlemen
With clever explanations of the way
Our diff'rent languages were born — and grew —
And spread to diff'rent corners of the earth,
But truth to tell, I find their theories dull.
None of their arguments appeals to me,
Stirs my imagination or evokes
A scene so full of human interest
As that set forth, briefly in Genesis.

"Let's think about it in a serious way:
Picture a thousand men — possibly more —
Engaged on an important building scheme
Raising a mighty tower to reach the skies.
They make the bricks and lay them carefully
Using a plummet line to get them straight;
The tower must be a first rate piece of work.
They all know this and do their level best,
Working in harmony at their appointed tasks.
So, day by day, the solid walls go up.

"Then suddenly, a horrid thing occurred
A strange disaster no one could foresee,
They found they could not speak each other's tongue
Nor understand each other's simplest word.

" 'Give me that hammer, Jack,' But Jack, alas!
Takes not the slightest heed of the request.
Tom says it louder — shouts — but all he gets
Is babbled nonsense from his dearest friend.
They curse, they swear — but neither understands.
The fight begins, they knock each other down,
And then, in rising wrath, they drew their knives . . .

"Alas, these two are not the only men
To shout and yell and quarrel with their friends.
Soon all the workers are at loggerheads,
The tower becomes a hideous battlefield.
Many are wounded in the senseless fray
While others scream in agony . . . and die.

137

"A sudden panic seizes all the rest;
They look around in horror at their work
What have they done? Oh, heavens, what *have* they done!
A curse is on this place! A dreadful curse!
They throw away their knives. They turn and fly —
Fly for their lives to north, south, east and west.

"The tower, half-built, begins to tumble down,
But yesterday it was a busy scene —
It was a very hive of industry —
Tonight stands empty, silent beneath the moon,
A haunt of jackals — yes — and vultures too!
And then an owl flies by on noiseless wings,
Alights upon a piece of masonry
And gives a dismal screech to call her mate . . ."

MINK AND DIAMONDS

The story-teller paused and wiped his brow.
"Edward," I said to him in breathless voice.
"The tale is just a myth — we all know that —
Yet you have made it real. It's come alive!
Oh, Edward, you could write! You have the Gift!"

"Sometimes I've thought the same myself," said he.
"But writing is hard work, Cecilia,
And I'm too lazy — that's the trouble — see?
This story, tho' so ancient and so strange,
Is up to date in a peculiar way,

For men are just the same; they have not changed—"
"They have not changed?" I asked.
                                    "No, not a whit!
Wars could begin in just the same mad way.

"This ancient story which I have retold
With several small additions of my own,
Could well be written as a modern play,
Used as a warning to the modern world,
Or, as the background for a thrilling plot,
It might be filmed in Hollywood.

"Hurrah! Yes, that's the very thing!" he cried.
"I've got some bright ideas! I'll write the script
And I'll produce a Technicolour Film,
The film will be a staggering Success,
The most Astounding Drama of the Year
I'll make a million dollars — if not more!

"I must engage an All-Star Cast, of course:
The Varley boys must be the Junior Leads
And Mrs. Leake the Villain of the Piece.
Sweet Mary Trevor and Cecilia Dale
Shall be Twin Stars at ninety pounds a week.
They must be clad quite suitably, in mink
And diamonds — and pearls as big as peas — "

"Edward, you're mad!" cried Mary. "I shall have
Most awful nightmares when I go to sleep."
"Sweet dreams," said Edward, solemn as a Judge.

"Sweet dreams you'll have, of far-off Hollywood,
Of dollars raining from the starry skies,
Of mink and pearls and glist'ning diamonds.
Then you'll awake and find yourself in Wick;
Find that your husband is the vicar there,
With not a single dollar to his purse!
Find that your winter coat is made of tweed,
Find that the Mothers in the Parish Hall,
Meeting as usual for their Sewing Bee,
Have suddenly become a raging mob
And cannot understand each other's speech."

"Oh, Edward, don't!" cried Mary in dismay.

And then we laughed. We laughed and laughed and
                                    laughed!
And then, still giggling, went upstairs to bed. . .

SOCIAL OCCASIONS

Mary had many kindly friends in Wick
And in the country places round about
Who liked to entertain their vicar's wife.

Parties were not at all in Mary's line —
She much preferred tea and a quiet chat
Beside the parlour fire. Her trouble was
She could not tell a lie — however white!
So, if they asked her, she was bound to go

Unless she had an adequate excuse.
Sometimes I went with Mary, sometimes found
I had 'a previous date' and stayed at home.

We visited the Hammertons for lunch,
The Bunches came to supper once or twice
And once or twice, we went to tea with them.
They lived a mile from Wick at Lister Hall.

Professor Bunch, his daughter Caroline
And Jack his son who was a Naval man,
But home on leave after a spell abroad,

Professor Bunch was very fond of chess
And very good at it — he'd played a lot.
The vicar was the only man in Wick
Who was a foeman worthy of his steel;
Sometimes their battles lasted half the night!

We called on old Miss Fynch, a lonely soul
Who had a flat above the grocer's shop.
She welcomed us with warmth and gave us tea
And asked us earnestly to come again.

We went to tea with other folk as well:
Parishioners belonging to the church.

Dear Lady Dunscombe at the Manor House
Asked us to lunch, not once but several times —
That was a little party we enjoyed!

She showed us pictures in her studio:
Some were just sketches, others finished work,
But all displayed her wondrous taste and skill.
She'd studied under painters of renown
In London and Paris but retained
Her own originality of style.

The flower-paintings were the best of all:
Roses and tulips, lilies in stately jars
And little porcelain bowls of scented herbs.
Each one a poem, exquisitely wrought
Poems in colour, to delight the eye!

MY NEW FRIEND

One day when Mary's time was not her own
(She had a Mothers' Meeting to attend)
I went to Lady Dunscombe's by myself.
She took me to her studio to see
A flower painting — her most recent work —
A Dresden jar of rose-red peonies.
It was not finished yet, but none the less,
It was a gorgeous thing; it struck the eye,
It held me spell-bound, rooted to the floor!

"You like it, I can see, Cecilia,"
Said Lady Dunscombe in doubtful voice.
"I feel the colours are a little bright — "
"Oh, Lady Dunscombe, no!" I cried. "Oh no!

The colouring is lovely. It's a dream!
True it is different from your other work
But please, please finish it — I'm sure you can."
She sighed and said, "It can't be finished, dear,
The paeonies have faded in the night.
My subjects are short-lived, they pine and droop
The petals fall and wither on the floor.

"My husband used to say, 'Why don't you take
A different subject for your busy brush?'
Sometimes I do, of course," said Lady D.
"Orders for portraits sometimes come my way —
And these are interesting, I admit,
But, best of all I love to work with flow'rs.
Each flower is a 'portrait' in my eyes,
No two alike in colour or in form
And so I can't replace them when they fade
I must abandon them — and start afresh."

Later, when we sat down to have our tea,
My hostess told me of her married life:
Her husband had enjoyed the social round
Meeting new people, entertaining them,
Going to races, theatres and balls.
The London Season was a busy time.
"No time for painting then!" the lady said,
And smiled, a little sadly at the thought.

At other times Lord Dunscombe liked to fly
To Italy and spend a month in Rome.

Cruises to distant lands were his delight:
Twice they had been to South America
And, round the Cape, to Chile and Peru.
She told me stories of adventures there
Amusing tales of what they'd seen and done
Told me about the many friends they'd made
Amongst the people of those distant lands.
And then she sighed and said "I've talked too much
And you have listened with a ready ear,
But now it is your turn. I want to know
What you have seen and done, Cecilia dear."

My tongue was tied — I could not say a word —
I had no adventures such as hers!
But Lady Dunscombe was encouraging
And soon I found that I had lost my fear —
I found that I could talk to her with ease.

She asked if I were kin to Hubert Dale —
He was a painter whom she much admired.
"Oh yes, he was my father," I replied.
"He taught me all he could, taught me to draw,
Taught me to use my colours and to paint.
I could not paint fine pictures, such as his,
But I'd a little talent of my own —
'Twas an unusual talent, very rare,
He found I had a vivid memory — "

Her ladyship exclaimed. "It is indeed
A most unusual thing — a precious Gift!"

"Father developed it. He made me look
At scenes in daily life. 'Cecilia, LOOK!
Cecilia use your eyes!' That's what he said.
He showed me how to use my Seeing Eye
And helped me to remember what I'd seen.

"At first I had to make a few brief notes
And hurry home to draw my little sketch
Before the subject faded from my mind
But very soon there was no need for haste,
Soon it became a habit . . . and a joy.
Soon it became the mainspring of my life.

"Alas, my father died . . . I was alone.
I grieved when he had gone: he was so dear,
He was so wonderful, so wise and true
We understood each other's every thought.
I grieved when he had gone but still I knew
He had not gone so very far away:
He still encouraged me. I heard his voice —
'Cecilia look! Cecilia use your eyes!'

"Where'er I went, in London or abroad,
I looked — I saw — remembered what I'd seen
And made the little sketches in my book.
Although so slight, these things were saleable;
I sold some through my agents, '*Plume and Preen*.'"

I paused and then I said, "It's . . . over now . . .
My Seeing Eye . . . has gone. I've tried . . . and tried . . ."

"That's not the way," her ladyship replied.
"My dearest child, you must not fret and fume,
You must not struggle to regain your skill.
There comes a time in everybody's life
When all the world seems profitless and stale,
Colours grow dim and inspirations fail
Ah then — I know it well — our only hope
Is to accept the trouble on our knees
And leave the future in the Hands of God.

"You have been ill," her ladyship declared.
"You think you're better but it's my belief
You're worrying too much, forcing yourself
To take an active part in daily life.
You should be resting, building up your strength;
That is the way to climb the stony path
And gain the summit of the hill to health."

"Thank you," I said . . . and meekly bowed my head.
I knew that every word she said was true.

That day — it was a happy day for me —
I made a friend for life, a loyal friend,
A friend whom I could honour and admire.

MARY'S GARDEN

The high-walled garden at the vicarage
Was sheltered from the wind. Here Mary's flowers

Thrived. Here Mary's guest (wrapped up in rugs)
Lay in a *chaise longue* and took her ease
And read and dreamed and climbed the hill to health.

Mary was busy with domestic chores
And other duties of a vicar's wife,
But sometimes came with coffee on a tray
And sat and chatted, resting for a while.
"If it could always be like this!" she said.
"Edward and I could be so happy here."

Then presently she sighed and told me more:
"The summer, here, is a distressing time
The trippers come in buses from afar:
They come on Sunday mornings when the bells
Are ringing out for Matins — but they pass . . .
Fathers and Mothers with their little ones,
Young men and girls, arms round each other's waists,
Chattering like starlings they go by.

The church means nothing to them," Mary said.
"And yet they are God's children, every one.
God's children streaming past their Father's door,
To eat and drink and play upon the shore.

"The days are long. Could they not spare one hour
From worldly pleasures? Do they never think
Of him who made the sunshine and the sea?
Who gave them health and strength to frolic here?
Could they not spare one hour to sing His praise?"

Alas, I found no answer to her plaint,
Partly because her sorrow was too deep
For me to soothe with easy sophistry;
Partly because I, too, had lapsed from grace
And taken Sunday as a day of play.

THE FALL

November now, but still the days were mild,
The sunshine gentle as an angel's kiss
And one by one the leaves began to fall,
Loosening their hold upon the spreading trees
Where they had hung all summer, drifting down
And settling quietly upon the ground.

'Pestilence-stricken multitudes'? Ah no!
These leaves were not like Shelley's, driven in fear
Before a base enchanter's senseless rage,
These leaves had still a duty to perform:
By dying to enrich their native land.

Slowly they fell, softly as flakes of snow,
Nestling amongst the bushes near the gate
Or on the flower bed beside the path,
Each went to rest on its appointed heap
Happily as an over-weary child
Lies down upon his bed and goes to sleep.

THE ROYAL GIFT

It was a lovely peaceful thing to see,
And so I watched it happen hour by hour
Until a beech leaf, caught in vagrant airs
Drifted across the lichen-covered wall,
And fell upon my hand . . .

                         It was so light
It was so small, so wonderfully made
It was a present fitted for a queen.

"Listen, Cecilia," said its Royal Sire.
"My wealth exceeds ten thousand such as this,
This gift is but a token from my store
To bring you comfort in your climb to health
To cheer you on your way and soothe your fear.
Rest in the Lord, wait patiently for Him,
And, lo, in His good time, you shall be giv'n
Your heart's desire. Again I tell you Rest . . .
And you shall find your talent is restored.

"This is your winter-time, your time for rest.
'Tis mine as well, but I — I have no fear.
Patient I wait the coming of the Spring.
Each year I spread my branches wide; each year
In Spring my green and tender leaves unfold
To give a welcome shade in Summer's heat.

"The gentle cows enjoy my leafy screen
They gather round — and stand — and chew the cud.

With heavy udders and slow-waving tails
They patiently await their milking-hour.
Birds roost amongst my interlacing twigs
And fashion nests in which to lay their eggs.
Roofed by my leaves, hidden from owl and hawk
They rear their young in sweet security.

"But now the sun's ray are no longer fierce,
The cows are safely byred, the nestlings flown
And I am tired so I must rest awhile
And seek refreshment for another Spring.
My spent leaves fall. Their work has been well done
Take courage from my tale . . ."
                                        When I awoke
The copper-coloured leaf was in my hand
And Edward, sitting on the grass, close by,
Looked up and said, "It was a happy dream —
Your eyes were closed, your lips were curved in smiles,
But now the sun had sunk behind the trees
And it is time for tea".
                                        So good they were
So kind and thoughtful that the ready tears
Flooded my eyes, "Edward, I'm stronger now
And so . . . and so I'd like to come to church.
I am a Prodigal, I've eaten husks,
But found no nourishment. May I come back?"

Smilingly he replied, "Not 'Prodigal'.
Riotous living has not been your sin.
You are a wayward child, Cecilia Dale,

150

A straying lamb, lost in the wilderness,
Alone and wand'ring in a barren place.
But now, thank God, you've found the Pilgrim Path
To lead you home. Surely you need not ask
If you'll be welcome in your Father's house?
The door is never shut to those who knock."

ST. MATTHEW'S CHURCH

St. Matthew's Church was old — a holy place,
A simple building in the Norman style
With barrel roof and niches in the walls.
The arching windows glowed with coloured glass
And shafts of light made patterns on the aisle.

It was the centre of the Trevors' lives:
Here Mary came, bringing her choicest flow'rs
To deck the altar; here she knelt and prayed.
Here Edward Trevor, in his proper sphere,
Seemed taller, nobler, sterner than his wont.
No longer Mary's well-beloved child
But verily the servant of the Lord.
Proud of his calling, gentle yet firm his mien,
His simple faith shone forth in every word.
And here came I, who had been lost awhile
But now was found — and happy in the fold.

Early on Sunday mornings in the dark
We climbed the path which led between the trees:

It was a stony pathway to the church
And very long and steep it was to me —
Two or three times I had to stop and rest.
Then, as we neared St. Matthew's, we could see
The lighted windows shine like coloured gems
And hear the music of the harmonious bells.

This path was private to the vicarage,
The main approach was from the other side:
Through the old lychgate, through the arching doors
Came old Miss Exley, Mr. And Mrs. Hood,
Colonel and Mrs. Hammerton, Miss Fynch,
Professor Bunch, his daughter Caroline,
And always, wet or fine, Jane Puddifat —
These were the faithful few.

                                    Others there were
Who sometimes came and sometimes stayed at home.

JANE PUDDIFAT.

Dear Mrs. Puddifat was small and thin,
She took in washing for her livelihood
And, white as snow, it danced upon her lines.
I'd heard about her — all that Mary knew
Which was not very much when all was said!
Her little cottage was by the churchyard wall
Sheltered five children — three were teenagers,
Already bigger than their tiny mum.

Three years ago, with all her little brood,
Jane Puddifat had come to Wick-on-Sea:
A mystery woman from the outside world,
A nine days' wonder to the village folk!
Where had she come from? They would like to know.
Why had she come to settle in their midst?
Was Mister Puddifat alive or dead?
And, if alive, then where (oh where) was he?
Jane never told. Though she was good and kind
And always ready to oblige a friend
With loans of tea or sugar from her store
And ever-ready help in times of need,
She kept the secrets of her married life
Beneath her neatly-parted raven hair.

Yes, even Mrs. Leake, who liked to probe
The inner secrets of her neighbours' lives
And leak them out to cronies over cups
Of strong-brewed tea, had failed in her attempt
To learn the secret history of Jane.

"Where have you come from, Mrs Puddifat?"
This, Mrs. Leake, with a beguiling smile.
And Jane replied, "From London, Mrs. Leake."
"From London? Oh! Why did you leave the town?"
"The country's better for the children's health."
"You'll find it dull at Wick?" "Oh no," said Jane,
"I have my work to do. I love my work.
It's nice to see my washing dying clean
In fresh sea-breezes, free from smuts and fog."

"But Wick is so remote. Why come to Wick?"
"Why not?" asked naughty Jane in mild surprise.
"This cottage was available and so
I hired a van and moved without delay."
"You won't stay long," suggested Mrs. Leake,
Shaking her head in melancholy style.
"Oh, we have settled down! We're happy here
With pleasant neighbours in the village street.
The children like to play upon the shore . . .
And Mike, my eldest boy, has got a job
At Mister Higginbotham's dairy farm."

Strangely enough not even Mrs. Leake
Had cheek enough to mention Mister P.
To ask outright if he were still extant
And why he had not come to Wick-on-Sea. . .

Reluctantly she turned and walked away.

Jane watched her neighbour's slow retreating back
Then, laughing softly, took the heated iron,
Spread the vicar's surplice on her board
And got to work again.
                              "But Edward knows"
Said Mary thoughtfully. "Yes, Edward knows.
She must have told her troubles when she came
I'm sure he knows the secrets of her past:
He treats her in a 'special' sort of way
And often says 'We must be kind to Jane' . . .
As if he were not kind to everyone!"

THE HOLLY AND THE IVY

Christmas at Wick and I was gaining strength;
There was elastic in my quickened step.
The path between the trees which led to Church
Was shorter now and easier to climb.
The weather had been wonderfully mild.

On Tuesday morning — it was Christmas Eve —
Mary and I and Mrs. Puddifat
Met by appointment at St. Matthew's door
And started decorations in the Church.

Then others came with late chrysanthemums,
Michaelmas daisies, trails of ivy leaves
And sprays of copper beech, preserved in jars.
Miss Exley brought a 'crib' that she had made
With little figures clustered round a stall.
Miss Fynch brought bowls of Roman hyacinths
And Mrs. Bodger variegated leaves
Her son had sent from Kew.
                              "What riches here!"
Cried Mary Trevor with a sparkling eye.
"No frost this year," said Mrs. Hammerton.
(Her mode of speech was brusque). She added, "Look!
Here is the holly. I've got visitors.
I have no time to decorate the church.
Miss Dale can do the pulpit, I suppose?"
Meekly I promised I would do my best.
"Nobody should do less," was the reply.

"Nobody can do more — that's very sure,"
Whispered Jane Puddifat, the kindly soul.
"I'll help you, Miss. These gold chrysanthemums
With sprays of copper beech will look a treat
In biggish jars against the old grey stone."

The work went briskly after that:
Young Hilda brought a ladder and some string
And twined the ivy round the window frames
With sprigs of scarlet holly here and there.

More flowers arrived. Then Lady Dunscombe came
With arum lilies from her green-houses —
These for the altar vases were designed.
Mary and Mrs. Hood and Mrs. Bouse
Chose pink and white carnations for the font.
It was a busy scene, a happy scene:
The hum of quiet voices filled the air.

Lastly the vicar came with tactful praise —
"How beautiful!" he cried. "Our dear old church
Has put on festal garb to greet her King!
This is indeed a transformation scene."

"As good as last year, Edward?" asked his wife
In anxious tones.
                    "Oh, better far!
"Last year I thought it rather overdone —
Too many flow'rs and too much greenery.
This year it's more artistic and restrained."

He turned to me and murmured an aside:
"Last year the doughty Mrs. Hammerton
Made a *cheval-de-frise* with holly leaves
And scarlet berries on the pulpit ledge.
One must admire her courage, I suppose."
"She had her gloves, sir. Leather gloves," said Jane.
Ruefully he replied, "But I had none."

Then turning to Miss Fynch, "Your hyacinths
Are always good. This year the best I've seen.
What perfect blooms! What a delicious scent!"
Blushing with pleasure, old Miss Fynch replied,
"Tom Bodger came and helped me plant the bulbs
And gave me good advice. He is so kind!
To him the praise is due and not to me."
"Yours was the daily care," the vicar said,
And left her, happy as a favoured child.

COME, ALL YE FAITHFUL

Then, at seven o'clock on Christmas morn
The merry bells rang out to welcome us
Old folk and young to worship at the shrine.
To bow the knee and sing the well-known hymns
And listen to the vicar's Christmas Talk . . .
My heart was full of happiness and peace.

I'd heard about the Varley boys — and now
I saw them singing in St. Matthew's choir.

They sat together, sharing all their books
And sang the Christmas hymns in cheerful tones.
They were so strong, so full of radiant health
It was a joy to see the handsome pair . . .
And they were so alike that you might think
You saw one boy, twice over, sitting there.

Their usual practice, when they came to church,
Was to leave Vi on duty at the farm.
She was a splendid watch-dog, big and strong,
Her bark was menacing, her growl was fierce,
In aspect she was ugly as a lion —
A terrifying sight to evil men
Who came to Elderberry Farm on mischief bent!

But sometimes Violet, sociably inclined,
Followed her masters all the way to Wick
And then they had to leave her, safely housed,
With Mr. Bouse the butcher and his wife —
Oh, she was quite content to stay with them!
Doubtless she knew she'd get a knuckle bone,
Or some such delicacy as a treat.

THE OLD OLD STORY

On Christmas morning, coming out of church
An unexpected vision met our eyes:
'Twas Bobby Bouse and Vi beneath the trees,
Sitting together on a mossy stone.

Her head was on his shoulder, Bobby's arms
Lovingly clasped around the creature's neck
And little Bobby — so it did appear —
Was murmuring sweet nothings in her ear.

"Oh! Just look at that!" cried Jim to Tim
(Or maybe Tim to Jim. I could not tell).
"Yes, it's 'A Case'" the other said, and smiled.

"What were you telling Vi?" enquired Miss Fynch
Smiling in friendly manner at the child.
"About the baby," Bobby Bouse replied.
"About the stable and the morning star
And angels singing to the shepherd boys."

Somebody laughed. It might have been Jed Smart
The grocer's son (who seemed to think himself
A cut above his neighbours in the place).

"Oh, you may laugh" said Bob defiantly.
"Vi *liked* the story. Listened to every word —
Vi understands all that I say to her!"

"I'm sure she understands," the vicar said,
And on his shoulder laid a gentle hand.

'Twas then, quite suddenly I felt the urge
To sketch the little scene before my eyes:
The lovely child and the ferocious beast
So happy in each other's company.

It was the first faint stirring of the Gift
Which I had thought gone for evermore.
And, very faint and very far away,
I heard the murmur of a well-known voice:
"Cecilia, look! Cecilia, use your eyes . . ."

WAR POEMS

Written 1911 - 1918

THE CRYSTAL GAZER

You brought a crystal globe and bid me gaze
That I might view the scenes of future days,
But, oh, I would to Heaven I had died
E'er I had torn the blissful veil aside.
How can I bear to tell you what I see?
Nothing on earth but tears is left to me
For all the future, filled with sobs and cries
Is spread before my horror-stricken eyes.

The whole wide world is bathed in bloody war,
Ne'r has such dreadful carnage been before.
By day and night, by sky and sea and land,
Man goes wide-eyed with murder in his hand.
I hear, beneath the awful din of guns,
A million mothers weeping for their sons.
The sound of wailing is on every side,
It is as if the very breezes cried!

I see a town, filled with a frightened crowd,
I hear guns firing nearer and more loud —
A crash! See over there a house is down,
The hostile guns are levelled on the town.
Wild cries I hear of grief and rage and pain,
They die away and all is still again.
A horde of children—most of whom are nude,
Invade the debris searching for some food.

Those in the town are dulled by want and fear,
Some run about, some cower in the rear.
Thin starving women creep about the street
Half-clothed, with no boots upon their feet.
No man is to be seen, the very boys
Have gone to war and put away their toys.
No home is sacred, every law is dead,
And one long wailing cry goes up for bread.

Night falls, and in the valley far below
A thousand camp-fires spread their crimson glow
Among the hills, which to the eastward lie,
Flames tower threateningly towards the sky
And from the blazing villages there comes
A stream of peasants, flying from their homes.
Old men bewildered, little children tired,
Women all weeping, burdened and bemired.

I see some dark-cloaked women from the town
Toward the battlefield go quietly down.
The dead and dying lie on every side,
Old men and young—and many mothers' pride.
In trembling grief, from group to group they go,
And, as the lanterns on the faces glow,
Each searching woman sees 'tis not her love
And breathes a grateful prayer to One Above.

At length they find a cannon in a space,
A man is with it—lying on his face.
They turn him over—very gently, too—
And then, Oh dearest love, I see 'tis you.
Oh Heaven, what an ending to my quest!
I see the warm blood flowing from your breast.
You face is very still, but, oh, my love,
I see your cold grey lips just gently move.

You speak, you speak, and call me by my name,
And whisper, "Dear, war is a cruel game!"
I see myself as by your side I kneel,
The lantern shining on the cannon's wheel.
Calling your name—but no, your soul has gone,
Winging its way toward the dark grey dawn.
A chill sweet smile upon your face appears
And then mine eyes are blinded by these tears.

THE CIVILIAN'S WIFE

I could not bid him go and fight
He was so dear—oh, he must stay,
I watched him, secretly each night,
And saw him off to work each day.

He must not go—it was my dread,
Swiftly I pictured life alone,
The struggle for my daily bread
And every joy in living gone.

We did not meet each other's eye
And spoke no word of what became
A nightmare to us—till I die
I shall remember all the shame.

Then as the days went by and War
Loomed large and fearsome in our eyes,
A fear, more awful than before
Seized on my heart will dull surprise.

I fixed my mind on food, on rent,
And yet I could not bear to see
My man at home, safe and content,
Whilst others fought for him and me.

When with a trembling voice and low
I spoke to him about the War,
I found he'd always longed to go
But feared to mention it before.

To leave me poor and all alone,
This was his fear—oh, what was right?
And though my heart was like a stone
I smiled, and bid him go and fight.

THE SOLDIER'S WIFE

War declared, the beating of a drum
The men cheered up—"By Heav'n our chance has
                                    come.

A European War at last, by Gad
We're lucky, but the Germans must be mad!
'How to get out before it's over—Eh!?"
We women shivered. Women have no say
In war, for if they had all war would cease.
The women pay in war, the men in peace.

Still, we were "soldiers' wives", we acted parts,
Talked rather big, cov'ring our sinking hearts.
We only then began to realise
That our men had been bought for sacrifice.

Those farewell dinners! God! When the champagne
Seemed choking us. The ghastly tearing pain
That gripped our throats, e'en when our pale lips
                                    smiled,
And jests were light, and conversation wild.

168

Then came a nightmare to which Hell were bliss:
The train, the handclasps and that one last kiss,
A kiss that seemed to tear our hearts, and then
The train swept out, bearing away our men.
And all we women in our pain were one
Though some of us had tears, and some had none.

AN ECHO OF THE WAR
IN A
HUMAN HEART

Spring 1918

God has sent Spring, leaves dancing in the sunshine,
Lambs playing on the hillside and the meads,
And children singing in the village gardens
And in the fields green tips to all the seeds.

God has made merry waves upon on the foreshore
And set wee birds to twitter in the lime,
Yes, Spring is spreading, spreading o'er the meadows
But Winter is in *my* heart all the time.

170

THE
HONOURABLE
LADY

THE HONOURABLE LADY

SCENE: The Totem Tea Shop.

Cast in order of appearance:
MRS McTAGGART, Proprietrix of the Tea Shop.
DAPHNE, her daughter (slightly simple)
MISS TOD
MRS SIMPSON
MISS CLARKE
MRS MAXTON
MR TOD

(The curtain rises disclosing the teashop with three tables, two doors and a window. MRS McTAGGART is discovered preparing the tables for tea. She is very capable and businesslike. She is dressed plainly but well, in outdoor clothes. She is obviously in a hurry)

MRS McT: *Raising voice:* Daphne. Daphne, are ye there. Will ye come here at once and lend a hand with the tables. Daphne!

DAPHNE: *Enters, looking untidy and flustered:* I couldna' find ma new apron. Will this do?

MRS McT: It's no very clean.

DAPHNE: It's the only one I could find. Will it do, mither?

MRS McT: It'll need to. I've no time to look for yer apron. See here noo—and mind what I'm telling ye—yon table by the window is for Mrs Simpson. There's three of them coming. They'll be here when the marriage is over. The other tables are for casuals. Folks may drift in after the marriage if they've no been asked to the reception. You'll need to keep the kettle on the boil.

DAPHNE: *Looking out of the indoor, suddenly and excitedly:* Mither! They're coming out noo—Oh my, there's the bride—all in white wi' a lace veil—and there's the man. He's a fine, upstanding fellow and no mistake—an the wee bridesmaid . . .

MRS McT: *Hesitating, but unable to resist the lure, goes to the window and peers out:* Aye, there they are. Man and wife for better or worse   Let's hope it's not worse . . .

DAPHNE: She looks real nice.

MRS McT: Aye, she's not bad at all. Mrs Strang looks like a pin-cushion in yon violet silk . . . and there's Mrs Simpson all togged up in magenta, with a sable cape.

DAPHNE: Where? Oh, aye, I see her noo. Is she not

asked to the reception?

MRS McT: I've told ye she's coming here to her tea, and Miss Clarke and Mrs Maxton forebye.

DAPHNE: Were they not asked to the reception, Mither?

MRS McT: *Irritably:* They're not going, anyway. Maybe they thought they'd get a better tea here. They will too. There's that chocolate cake—one piece each and nae mair—mind that, Daphne.

DAPHNE: Who's that in the pink hat? She's nice looking, Mither.

MRS McT: That's the county surveyor's daughter.

DAPHNE: *Amazed:* The Countess of Ayr's daughter!

MRS McT: That's what I said. Now see here, Daphne. You'll need to keep your wits aboot ye. Dinna forget tae put tea in the teapot like you did last time Mrs Simpson was here. And for maircy's sake remember to take the money — one and sixpence each. *Seizes her bag and gloves and prepares to depart.* Are ye listening, Daphne. Daphne, d'ye hear me?

DAPHNE: *Awaking from her dream:* Aye, I'm listening. I'll mind all ye say. I'll manage fine.

MRS McT: You'll manage fine if you dinna get reading yon silly book about Lady Cynthia, or whatever it is. If you get your nose into that there's no knowing what you'll do.

DAPHNE: I'll not read a wurrd of it, I promise.

Exit MRS McTAGGART by the street door

MRS McT: *As she goes:* Mind what I've told ye, Daphne—I'll not be late. Keep the kettle on the boil . . .

DAPHNE sees her off and then flies back to the window

DAPHNEI   My, what a lot of folks—and all in their Sunday best. There's the lady in the pink hat. Her Mither's a Countess. It wud be grand to have a Countess for yer mither. She'll be an "Honourable" like Miss Fotheringay in the book. Yon's a nice hat, she's got—but ye could have any amount of nice hats if yer mither was a countess . . . Guid sakes, she's coming here. *Excitedly* Aye, she's making straight for the door. Guid sakes I wish I had ma new apron.

176

Rushes to the mirror and tries to tidy her hair.

Enter MISS TOD, very smartly dressed for the wedding and wearing the pink hat admired by DAPHNE. She looks round.

MISS TOD: Can I have tea here?

DAPHNE: *All of a fluster:* Aye, ye can that—and you'll get a better tea than ye would at the reception.

MISS TOD: *Smiling:* Have you cakes and scones?

DAPHNE: Any amount. Will I infuse the tea noo?

MISS TOD: Not yet. I must go and find my father and tell him to call for me on his way back. I shan't be long.

DAPHNE: *With interest:* Is he to be at the reception, then?

MISS TOD: Yes. *She points to the window table.* I'll sit there. I'll be back in a few minutes.

DAPHNE: Ye can't sit there, it's engaged—but maybe, *hesitates,* maybe as you're the Countess of Ayr's daughter—if that's what you are?

177

MISS TOD: *Smiling:* Yes, that's what I am.

DAPHNE: *Gazing at her:* D'ye like it?

MISS TOD: Like it? Yes, I think so. It might be worse.

DAPHNE: *With interest:* You'll be Honourable, then?

MISS TOD: *Humouring the creature:* Honourable — well, of course. Very honourable indeed. You can trust me not to steal the tea-spoons.

DAPHNE: *Shocked:* Och, I never thocht that. I was meaning you were an honourable lady.

MISS TOD: *Smiling:* Well, you've said it.

DAPHNE: Whit does it feel like?

MISS TOD: *Puzzled:* You mean what does it feel like to be honourable?

DAPHNE: *Nodding:* Aye, that's whit I meant.

MISS TOD: *Smiling:* Well, to tell you the truth it's rather a nuisance to be honourable these days. There are so many little wangles to be worked with coupons—clothes and petrol coupons—but of course you can't do that if you're honourable . . .

DAPHNE: *Breathlessly:* It's noblesse obleege.

MISS TOD: *Laughing:* Something like that, I suppose. *She goes towards the door.* You'll keep the table for me, won't you?

DAPHNE: *Emphatically:* I will that.

Exit MISS TOD by the street door. Exit DAPHNE by the other door into the back premises

Enter MRS SIMPSON and MISS CLARKE, both dressed up to the nines. MRS SIMPSON as described, with a fur cape.

MRS S: It went off very well, I thought. I didn't much care for the bridesmaids dresses of course. That particular shade of pink is so trying—it made the younger Strang girl look quite sallow.

MISS CLARKE: It's to be hoped the poor girl will be happy. Nobody seems to know much about him.

MRS S: *Taking off her gloves and sitting down at the window table.* He's a stockbroker or something—quite well off, I believe. Rather lucky to get anybody for that girl after the way she's behaved . . . running about all over the place with

MISS C: That's true, but all the same I didn't care for the look of him very much.

MRS S: What did you think of Clara Maxton's get up?

MISS C: *Smiling:* My dear.

MRS S: *Smiling:* I know. Poor Clara hasn't much taste, has she? That hat! *Throws off her cape.*

MISS C: More suitable for a girl of eighteen than a woman of her age with grown up sons.

While she is speaking the door opens and CLARA MAXTON enters, very smartly dressed with an ultra fashionable hat.

MRS S: *Loudly:* The other bridesmaid was his sister of course. Rather pretty I thought.

MRS MAXTON: Here I am. Couldn't get away before. That dreadful old Maior Brown got hold of me. Still talking about the wedding?

MISS C: *Slightly flustered:* Yes, we were just saying . . . What were we saying, Edna?

MRS S: *Firmly:* The bridesmaids' dresses—such an
            ugly colour, weren't they? Come and sit
            down, Clara, you look hot.

MRS M: (Taking off her gloves) Your usual table, I
            see.

MRS S: Mrs McTaggart knows I like this table. She
            always keeps it for me.

MISS C: We shall get a much better tea here than
            at the reception. The Strangs always do
            things on the cheap.

MRS S: *Nodding:* Mrs McTaggart's cakes are all
            home-made.

MRS M: *Sitting down and settling her hat:* How do
            you like it, Edna?

MRS S: *Looking at the hat which she has been
            criticising so severely—replies with great
            conviction:* Charming. Just right for a
            wedding. So gay.

MRS M: Not too gay, I hope. What do you think,
            Jane?

MISS C: *Without conviction and somewhat
            flustered:* Oh no not at all—I mean—not
            too gay for a wedding.

181

MRS M: I was doubtful about it you know, but the boys made me have it. I don't know when I shall ever wear it again. *Sighs.*

MISS C: Perhaps there will be another wedding soon.

MRS S &
MRS M: *Eagerly:* Whose?

MISS C: *Flustered again:* Oh nobody—I mean I just thought they say one wedding brings another, don't they?

Her companions look at her in some disgust and there is a short silence.

MRS M: *Turning to MRS SIMPSON:* You were saying you had a letter from your sister in Seatown.

MRS S: Oh yes—it's about those new people who have taken the Beeches. *Takes a letter from her bag.* Hm—yes, here it is . . . She says: "I don't think you will like the Tods very much. They were anything but popular in Seatown. He's not too bad, in fact quite a nice little man in his way—we were all rather sorry for him—but Mrs Tod is very ordinary, not your type at all. The family consists of two grown-up sons and a daughter . . . quite impossible, we thought. Rather fast and terribly pushing, hail fellow well-met with all and sundry. She pushed her way into everything here, and will probably do the same at Beckford if she gets a chance." *Folds up the letter.* What do you think of that?

MRS M: Frightful—simply frightful!

MISS C: We don't want people like that here.

MRS M: *Thoughtfully:* Forewarned is forearmed.

MRS S: *Nodding:* That's why I told you. I mean we can keep them in their place from the start. I'm determined not to have them in the Bridge Club.

MISS C: I should think not.

MRS M: Mr Tod has something to do with the County Council, Lionel said. I may have to call on them because, of course, Lionel is on the Council, but I shall take care not to get involved.

MISS C: *With a sigh:* What a pity, isn't it? We do want some more really nice people in Beckford. People who would be friendly and congenial. We could do with some new blood in the Dramatic Club . . .

MRS S: *Looking round:* Why don't they bring our
              tea, I wonder? *Sees the bell and rings it In
              a peremptory manner.*

Enter DAPHNE with a tray of cakes.

DAPHNE: *Nearly dropping the tray.* Guid sakes, it's
              you! It's you that rang!

MRS S: Who did you think it was, Daphne?

DAPHNE: I thocht it was her. I didn't know you'd
              come. You can't sit there.

MRS S: But I engaged this table yesterday.
              Where's your mother, Daphne?

DAPHNE   She's away to Peebles. She'll not be back
              till late. I'm doing the teas masel'. You'll
              have tae move, Mrs Simpson.

MRS S: But, Daphne, I engaged this table
              yesterday. Your mother said I could have
              it. You know quite well I always have this
              table.

DAPHNE: I know that fine, but there's an
              Honourable coming and she's wanting it.
              She'll be here any minute noo. I wonder
              she's no here already. Real nice she was,
              wit an awfu' neat wee hat.

MRS S: Who did you say she was?

DAPHNE: An Honourable. Her mither's a countess—
            think o' that!

MRS M: A countess—Are you sure?

DAPHNE: Aye, a countess—would her faither be a
            count, Mrs Simpson?

MRS S: *Doubtful:* Well . . .

MRS M: No, Daphne. Her father would be an earl.

DAPHNE   Guid sakes, think of that

There is a short silence.

MISS C: *Incredulously:* Do you mean she's coming
            here for tea?

DAPHNE: She is that. And I said she could have that
            table. I'll put you over there, you'll not
            mind for once?

*The three LADIES rise and begin to collect their
belongings. It takes them a little while to move and get
settled. Meanwhile DAPHNE goes out and returns with
the tea.*

MISS C: *In a low voice:* I wonder when she'll be
            back.

185

MRS M:	We needn't hurry.
MISS C:	No, we can dawdle over our tea.
MRS M:	Daphne said she wouldn't be long.
DAPHNE:	Just a few minutes she said. She's awfu' nice-looking mind you.
MRS S:	*Pouring out:* You take milk and sugar, don't you Clara? Jane takes sugar but no milk . . . is that right?

They state their preferences and are served with tea by their hostess. All three are somewhat subdued and keep glancing towards the door. DAPHNE goes out.

MISS C:	Was she at the wedding, I wonder.
MRS S:	Let me see—there was rather a nice-looking girl in a pink hat. She was sitting behind the MacDonalds . . .
MRS M:	I didn't see her, Edna.
MRS S:	No, you wouldn't. You were sitting further up. She's about the only possible . . . I mean I knew every one else.
MISS C:	There was rather a nice-looking woman with the bridegroom's mother.

MRS S: No, no. That's Mrs Hobson, the bride-
            groom's aunt.

MRS M: There was a small woman in grey with a
            diamond star. That might be the Countess,
            perhaps.

MISS C: Oh you mean sitting with the Strangs.
            She's a cousin of the Strangs . . . lives in
            Edinburgh. They introduced me to her
            yesterday. She was very disagreeable, I
            thought.

MRS S: I saw her. She came in a Rolls. Heaps of
            money, I suppose.

MRS M: I can't think of anyone else the least
            likely.

*There is a short silence. Enter DAPHNE with three pieces
of chocolate cake.*

DAPHNE: You're to get a piece of cake each and nae
            mair. *Puts the plate down.*

MISS C: One piece will be sufficient for me.

DAPHNE: Suddenly bursting out: Oh my, it's just
            awfu'! This would happen when ma
            mither's oot. I'll be sure tae dae
            something wrang an' then I'll get blamed.

187

I'm just all bamboozled wit it . . . an' I havena even a clean apron tae pit on.

MISS C: Come now Daphne. It's no use making a fuss. You will manage quite nicely if you keep calm. Keep calm—that's the great thing.

MRS M: She won't notice your apron. The real aristocracy are quite easy and natural. There's nothing to worry about.

DAPHNE: I wish I had ma hair permed.

MRS S: Make her a good cup of tea and be sure to heat the teapot first. That's more important than your hair.

MISS C: See that the water is absolutely boiling, Daphne.

Enter MISS TOD

DAPHNE: *In a loud whisper:* This is her.
Exit hastily

MISS TOD: *Walking over to her table and taking off her gloves:* What a lovely afternoon!

ALL THREE: *In chorus:* Yes indeed! Perfectly lovely! So warm and pleasant!

MISS TOD: But not too warm.

ALL THREE: No, not a bit too warm.

MISS TOD: Lucky for the wedding, isn't it?

MRS S: Very lucky indeed.

MISS C: It's a good thing the wedding wasn't yesterday, isn't it?

MRS M: Happy is the bride the sun shines on.

Enter DAPHNE with the tea pot. She puts it down in front of MISS TOD.

DAPHNE: Is that all? I mean are you wanting anything else?

MISS TOD: You haven't brought any milk.

DAPHNE: Guid sakes, neather I have.
               Rushes off.

MRS S: *Confidentially:* Her mother is away for the afternoon. Daphne is a little—well just a little . . .

MISS TOD: Batty, if you ask me. *Smiles.*

All THREE LADIES smile and nod.

MISS TOD: *Leans across and speaks confidentially:*
              She asked me if I were "honourable" and
              seemed very much impressed when I
              replied that I was—she asked what it felt
              like.

They all laugh. Enter DAPHNE with the milk jug.

DAPHNE: That's the top of the milk . . . and you can
              have two pieces of chocolate cake if you
              want.

MISS TOD: Thank you. I'm not sure I shall want more
              than one.

DAPHNE: Well, I'll just leave it in case.

Exit DAPHNE

MISS TOD: *Pouring out her tea:* She's a scream, isn't
              she?

MRS M: She's very simple poor thing. The last time
              we were here she forgot to put any tea in
              the teapot.

MISS TOD: How amusing.

MRS M: Yes, it was.

MISS TOD: Well, she's made up for it to-day. She

seems to have emptied half the tea-caddy into this pot.

MRS M: Has she given you any hot water? No? Really she is careless.

MRS S: *Looking into her hot water jug:* There's plenty here.

MISS C: *Takes jug and goes over to MISS TOD's table.* Strong tea has a very unpleasant taste, hasn't it?

MISS TOD: Thank you very much.

MISS C: *Lingering at MISS TOD's table:* You mustn't judge the tea shop by this afternoon. Mrs McTaggart herself is most capable, but she had to go to Peebles. She makes all the cakes herself—you can get excellent coffee here in the morning—elevenses, we call it. *Smiles.*

MISS TOD: That's worth knowing. I must certainly come here for my elevenses.

MISS C: Oh, you're staying in Beckford. I thought perhaps you had just come for the wedding.

MISS TOD: We're staying at the Grand Hotel until . . .

MISS C:	*Eagerly interrupting:* Oh, I'm so glad. I'm sure you'll like Beckford. It's a delightful place to live. I've lived here all my life so I ought to know. *Laughs.*
MISS TOD:	*Thoughtfully:* I wonder.
MISS C:	You wonder?
MISS TOD:	I wonder whether you really do know more about Beckford than—say somebody who has lived part of her life elsewhere.
MISS C:	But of course . . . I've had more time.
MRS M:	I think I know what you mean. *Smiles at MISS TOD.*
MISS TOD:	*Apologetically:* I just meant—you know the old saying "What can he know of Beckford that only Beckford knows."
MRS M:	*Nodding:* Quite.
MISS C:	Oh, I see what you mean now. But of course I've travelled quite a lot. I always go to England for my summer holidays.
MRS S:	*Breaking into the conversation: she is tired of being left out:* There is quite a lot going on in Beckford—you mustn't run away

with the idea that we're dull country folk. *Laughs.* There is tennis and dancing and riding and there's an excellent Picture House. Our young people seem to find plenty of amusement here.

MRS M: Yes, indeed. They're always on the go. I never seem to see my boys—if it's not one thing it's another.

MISS TOD: *Confidentially:* Dancing is what I like. I'd just go anywhere or do anything for a dance.

MRS S: There's a dance here tomorrow night at the Town Hall. (Hesitates) I wonder— would you care to go? It's a very primitive little affair of course . . .

MISS TOD: I should love to go. *Doubtfully:* But—but the only thing is I shouldn't know a soul, should I? It might be rather dull— knowing nobody, I mean

MRS S: That wouldn't matter, we could easily—

MRS M: *Dashing in before MRS SIMPSON:* You must come with us.

MISS TOD: *Amazed:* With you?

MRS M:	Yes do. It would be such a pleasure. We're having a little dinner beforehand—just a few young people, quite an informal sort of meal. It would be delightful if you would join us and go on to the dance with our party.
MISS TOD:	*Delighted:* But how kind. Are you sure?
MRS M:	*Nodding eagerly:* Of course. You must come. I shall look forward to having you.
MISS TOD:	That *is* kind of you.
MRS M:	*Taking a card out of her bag and going across to the other table:* I'm so glad I thought of it. Dinner is at 7.30—a ridiculously early hour, I'm afraid, but the dance begins at 9 o'clock. *Hands over the card.* Everyone knows our house . . .

They chat in undertones about their arrangements: MISS TOD says she will get a taxi etc. Meanwhile MRS SIMPSON is scrabbling in her bag, looking for something.

MISS C:	Have you lost your handkerchief, Edna?
MRS S:	*Irritably:* I'm looking for a card. I don't seem to have one—most annoying. Clara is terribly pushing, isn't she?

194

MISS C:	*Calmly:* I have no cards, and never had. To my mind they're quite absurd unless you're a commercial traveller or something.
MRS S:	I wanted to give her one—it's the right thing.
MISS C:	You can tell her your name, can't you?
MRS S:	She might forget.

The other conversation finishes and MRS MAXTON returns to her seat.

MRS S:	*Leaning forward and speaking across the room:* I wonder if you care for bridge.
MISS TOD:	Well, no—bridge isn't much in my line. Mother plays, of course.
MISS C:	*Persuasively:* Perhaps you're interested in Drama.
MISS TOD:	Drama?
MISS C:	We have a flourishing dramatic club in Beckford.
MISS TOD:	*Interested:* Now you're talking. I just love private theatricals. I've done quite a lot,

really. I like modern plays best—not Shakespeare.

MISS C: We're thinking of doing a Bridie play this season.

MISS T: How splendid. Could I—I mean can one join the club?

MISS C: Of course you can join—you must. I was just saying to Mrs Simpson we need new members. *Confidentially:* As a matter of fact people have to be proposed and seconded for election, but I don't think we need bother about that in your case. Everybody will be delighted to have you.

MISS TOD   *Surprised:* Really? How nice of them. *Hesitates.* This does surprise me.

MISS C: Surprise you?

MISS TOD: Yes. You see, *confidentially* I was told that Beckford was a frightfully sticky place.

MISS C: Sticky?

MISS TOD: *Nodding:* Frightfully sticky—cliquey, you know. They said it would take years to get to know anybody. I was rather dreading it to tell you the truth.

MISS C: But that's nonsense. Beckford isn't a bit
               like that.

MISS TOD: *Smiling:* No, I can see it isn't.

There is a short silence

MRS M: *In puzzled tone of voice:*   But surely
               people are always ready to be friendly
               with you, wherever you go.

MISS TOD: You mean I'm easy to get on with? Yes,
               that's true. I make friends very easily. I
               like to know everybody and be in things,
               if you know what I mean. My worst
               enemy couldn't call me a snob.

MISS C: *Emphatically:* No, indeed.

MRS S: *Complacently:* I can't bear snobs.

MRS M: *Earnestly:* But one must draw the line
               somewhere, of course.

MRS S: Oh, definitely.

*There is a short silence while the LADIES ponder upon
the exact place to draw the line. MISS TOD takes out her
compactum, makes up her lips and powders her nose.
While she is thus engaged the following conversation
takes place in low tones.*

MISS C: *In a whisper to MRS SIMPSON:*
             Delightful, isn't she? So unspoilt, I am glad
             I managed to get her for the Dramatic
             Club—

MRS S: Charming girl—quite an asset.

MRS M: The *real* aristocracy. How different from
             the modern upstarts. *Breeding*—that's
             what counts.

*Enter MR TOD. He is attired for the wedding and has a
flower in his button-hole.*

MR TOD: Ah, there you are, Millicent. *He looks
             around.* Quite a nice little place.

*Advances to his daughter's table without taking any
notice of the other ladies. The other ladies take no notice
of him, but chat in undertones to one another.*

MISS TOD: It's a *very* nice place, father. I've had an
             excellent tea.

MR TOD: More than we had. Very poor claret-cup
             and the cake was made of sawdust. Come
             along, we mustn't keep your mother
             waiting.

MISS TOD: *Rising and collecting bag etc.* Oh, I
             haven't paid. I had better ring for the girl.

Takes up little bell and rings it.

Enter DAPHNE with a large black kettle in her hand.

DAPHNE: Is it hot water you're wanting? I couldn't find the wee silver jug but this'll be hotter and—and . . .

MISS TOD: No, I've finished, thank you. How much is it?

MR TOD: I'll pay, I'll pay. *Takes a handful of silver out of his pocket.*

DAPHNE: *Gazing at him:* Is this yer faither? My, I've never seen an airl before.

MR TOD: What on earth does she mean. Eh?

MISS TOD: *Aside:* The poor thing's half-witted.

MR TOD: Oh, I see—poor soul. *To DAPHNE:* How much is it, my girl?

DAPHNE: *In a dream:* It's—it's one and sax—that is–

MR TOD: Well, here's half a crown. You can keep the change.

DAPHNE: *Taking it:* My, I wish there was more airls about.

199

MR TOD:	Kindly: There, that's right, isn't it? You can buy sweets with it—if you've any points left. *Pats her shoulder.*
MISS TOD:	*Hesitating:* Oh, father. I want to introduce you to these ladies. They've been so very kind and friendly. *To MRS MAXTON:* May I introduce my father—Mrs. er— *Looks at the card:* Mrs Maxton.
MRS M:	*Rising:* How d'you do. This is a great pleasure.
MR TOD:	Delighted. *They shake hands.* I think I know your husband—Colonel Maxton— he's on the County Council, isn't he?
MRS M:	*Flattered:* Oh yes—yes he is—yes.
MISS TOD:	Mrs Maxton has asked me to dinner tomorrow night—and to go to a dance
MR TOD:	Very kind, very kind—Millicent is quite mad on dancing.
MISS TOD:	And this is Mrs—er—
MRS S:	*Rising and holding out her hand:* Mrs Simpson is my name—and this is Miss Clarke. It has been such a pleasure to meet your daughter quite informally, like this.

MR TOD: *Proudly:* Millicent gets on with everybody.

MISS TOD: *Laughing:* You mean I get off with everybody, father.

MR TOD: *Laughing:* Well, perhaps—perhaps.

They all shake hands, laughing delightedly at the joke.

MISS TOD: Mrs Simpson runs the Bridge Club, father.

MR TOD: Hah, Bridge! That's more my line than dancing—ha ha. My wife is very keen, very keen.

MRS S: *Eagerly:* Perhaps you'd like to join the club?

MR TOD: Thank you—thank you. We shall be delighted—I can speak for my wife too. Put us both down, Mrs Simpson—Tod is the name.

MRS S: *In amazement:* Tod!

MR TOD: That's right, Tod. Tod with one D.

Mrs SIMPSON gazes at him incredulously

MR TOD: Mr and Mrs Alexander Tod. I'm the

County Surveyor, you know.

MRS S: You're the Countess of Ayr?

MR TOD: That's right.

MRS S: But how can a *man* be the Countess of
            Ayr?

MR TOD: *Surprised:* I never heard of a woman
            getting the job.

MRS S: *Faintly:* You never . . .

MR TOD: *Jocosely:*   There are ladies in most
            professions   nowadays—doctors   and
            lawyers and members of parliament and
            what not, but I've yet to hear of a lady
            being appointed County Surveyor.

*He hesitates, looking from one to the other. Their faces
are all blank. He continues in a more serious explaining
sort of tone.*

            I've just been appointed, you know. Mr
            Law retired—too old for the job—and
            they gave it to me.

MRS M: But what . . . I mean how . . .

MR TOD: *Smiling at her:* Well, you ask Colonel

Maxton. He knows all about it. As a matter of fact it was due largely to his influence that I got the job. I was Burgh Surveyor in Seatown before, but I think I'm going to like this job much better.

MISS C: *In horrified accents:* You mean you're the new County Surveyor?

MR TOD: That's what I told you.

MISS TOD: *With a pleased expression:* And we've got a house—it's called the Beeches. We're hoping to move in next week—and you must all come to a house-warming party. Mustn't they, father?

MR TOD: Of course, of course—directly we're settled—the sooner the better. My wife will be delighted to see you.

There is a short but pregnant silence

Continuing: Well, we mustn't keep mother waiting any longer. Come along, Millicent, say goodbye to your new friends.

MISS TOD: Goodbye—goodbye— *Shakes hands in turn with the three limp LADIES.* It's been so nice meeting you. I know I'm going to

like Beckford immensely. *To MRS
MAXTON:* Seven thirty tomorrow night.
I shan't forget.

*MR TOD smiles and bows, opens the door for his
daughter and they both go out.*

*The three LADIES are left standing in different positions,
frozen with dismay, as*

THE CURTAIN FALLS

AN AUTOBIOGRAPHICAL
SKETCH

AN AUTOBIOGRAPHICAL SKETCH

EDINBURGH was my birthplace and I lived there until I was married in 1916. My father was the grandson of Robert Stevenson who designed the Bell Rock Lighthouse and also a great many other lighthouses and harbours and other notable engineering works. My father was a first cousin of Robert Louis Stevenson and they often played together when they were boys.

So it was that from my earliest days I heard a good deal about "Louis", and, like Oliver Twist, I was always asking for more, teasing my father and my aunts for stories about him. He must have been a strange child, a dreamy unpredictable creature with a curious fascination about him which his cousins felt but did not understand. How could ordinary healthy, noisy children understand that solitary, sensitive soul! And as they grew up they understood him even less for Louis was not of their world. He was born too late or too early. The narrow conventional ideas of mid-Victorian Edinburgh were anathema to him. Louis would have been happy in a romantic age, striding the world in cloak and doublet with a sword at his side, he would have sold his life deerly for a Lost Cause—he was ever on the side of the under-dog. He might have been happy in the world of today when every man is entitled to his own opinions and the Four Freedoms is the goal of Democracy.

My father was old-fashioned in his ideas so my sister and I were not sent to school but were brought up at home and educated by a governess. I was always very fond of reading and read everything I could get hold of including Scott, Dickens, Jane Austen and all sorts of boys' books by Jules Verne and Ballantyne and Henty.

When I was eight years old I began to write stories and poems myself. It was most exciting to discover that I could. At first my family was amused and interested in my efforts but very soon they became bored beyond measure and told me it must stop. They said it was ruining my handwriting and wasting my time. I argued with them. What was handwriting for, if not to write? "For writing letters when you're older," they said. But I could not stop. My head was full of stories and they got lost if I did not write them down, so I found a place in the box-room between two large black trunks with a skylight overhead and I made a little nest where I would not be disturbed. There I sat for hours—and wrote and wrote.

Our house was in a broad street in Edinburgh—45 Melville Street—and at the top of the street was St. Mary's Cathedral. The bells used to echo and re-echo down the man-made canyon. My sister and I used to sit on the window-seat in the nursery (which was at the top of the house) and look down at the people passing by. I told her stories about them. Some of the memories of my childhood can be found in my novel, *Listening Valley,* in which Louise and Antonia had much the same lonely childhood.

Every summer we went to North Berwick for several months and here we were more free to do as we wanted, to go out by ourselves and play on the shore and meet other children. When we were at North Berwick we sometimes drove over to a big farm, close to the sea. We enjoyed these visits tremendously for there were so many things to do and see. We rode the pony and saw the farmyard animals and walked along the lovely sands. There were rocks there too, and many ships were wrecked upon the jagged reefs until a lighthouse was erected upon the Bass Rock—designed by my father. Years afterwards I wrote a novel about this farm, about the fine old house and the beautiful garden, and I called it *The Story of Rosabelle Shaw.*

As we grew older we made more friends. We had bathing picnics and tennis parties and fancy dress dances, and of course we played golf. I was in the team of the North Berwick Ladies' Golf Club and I played in the Scottish Ladies' Championship at Muirfield and survived until the semi-finals. I was asked to play in the Scottish Team but by that time I was married and expecting my first baby so I was obliged to refuse the honour.

Every Spring my father and mother took us abroad, to France or Switzerland or Italy. We had a French maid so we spoke French easily and fluently—if not very correctly —and it was very pleasant to be able to converse with the people we met. I liked Italy best, and especially Lake Como which seemed to me so beautiful as to be almost unreal. Paris came second in my affections. There was such a gay feeling in Paris; I see it always in sunshine with the white buildings and broad streets and the crowds of brightly clad people strolling in the Boulevards or sitting in the cafes eating and drinking and chattering cheerfully. Quite often we hired a carriage and drove through the Bois de Boulogne. My sister and I were never allowed to go out alone, of course, nor would our parents take us to a play—as I have said before they were old-fashioned and strict in their ideas and considered a "French Play" an unsuitable form of entertainment for their daughters—but in spite of these annoying prejudices we managed to have quite an amusing time and we always enjoyed our visits to foreign countries.

In 1913 I "came out" and had a gay winter in Edinburgh. There were brilliant "Balls" in those far off days, the old Assembly Rooms glittered with lights and the long gilt mirrors reflected girls in beautiful frocks and men in uniform or kilts. The older women sat round the ballroom attired in velvet or satin and diamonds watching the dancers—and especially watching their own offspring —with eyes like hawks, and talking scandal to one another. We danced waltzes and Scottish country dances and Reels—the Reels were usually made up beforehand by the Scottish Regiment which was quartered at Edinburgh Castle. It was a coveted honour to be asked to dance in these Reels and one had to be on ones toes all the time. Woe betide the unfortunate girl who put a foot wrong or failed to set to her partner at exactly the right moment!

The First Great War put an end to all these gaieties— certainly nobody felt inclined to dance when every day the long lists of casualties were published and the gay young men who had been ones partners were reported dead or missing or returned wounded from the ghastly battlefields.

In 1916 I married Major James Reid Peploe. His family was an Edinburgh family, as mine was. Curiously enough

I knew his mother and father and his brothers but had never met him until he returned to Edinburgh from the war, wounded in the head. When he recovered we were married and then began the busiest time of my life. We moved about from place to place (as soldiers and their wives and families must do) and, what with the struggle to get houses and the arrival—at reasonable intervals—of two sons and a daughter I had very little time for writing. I managed to write some short stories and some children's poems but it was not until we were settled for some years in Glasgow that I began my literary career in earnest.

Mrs Tim was my first successful novel. In it I wrote an account of the life of an Officer's wife and many of the incidents in the story are true—or only very slightly touched up. Unfortunately people in Glasgow were not very pleased with their portraits and became somewhat chilly in consequence. After that I wrote *Miss Buncle's Book* which has been one of my most popular books. It sold in thousands and is still selling. It is about a woman who wrote a book about the small town in which she lived and about the reactions of the community.

All the time my children were growing up I continued to write: *Miss Buncle Married*, *Miss Dean's Dilemma*, *Smouldering Fire*, *The Story of Rosabelle Shaw*, *The Baker's Daughter*, *Green Money*, *Rochester's Wife*, *A World in Spell* followed in due succession—and then came the Second Great War.

Hitherto I had written to please myself, to amuse myself and others, but now I realised that I could do good work. *The English Air* was my first novel to be written with a purpose. In this novel I tried to give an artistically true picture of how English people thought and felt about the war so that other countries might understand us better, and, judging by the hundreds of letters I received from people all over the world, I succeeded in my object—succeeded beyond my wildest hopes. My wartime books are *Mrs Tim Carries On, Spring Magic, Celia's House, Listening Valley, The Two Mrs Abbotts, Crooked Adam* and *The Four Graces.* In these books I have pictured every-day life in Britain during the war and have tried to show how ordinary people stood up to the frightfulness and what they thought and did during those awful years of anxiety. One of my American readers wrote to me and said, "You make us understand what it must be like to have a tiger in the backyard." I appreciated that letter.

Wartime brought terrible anxieties to me, for my elder son was in Malta during the worst of the Siege of that island and then came home and landed in France on D-Day and went through the whole campaign with the Guards Armoured Division. He was wounded in ten places and was decorated with the Military Cross for outstanding bravery. My daughter was an officer in the Women's Royal Naval Service and was commended for her valuable work.

In addition to my writing I organised the collection of Sphagnum Moss for the Red Cross and together with others went out on the moors in all weathers, wading deep in bog, to collect the moss for surgical dressings. This particular form of war-work is described in detail in *Listening Valley.*

After the long weary years of war came victory for the

Allies, but my job of writing stories went on. I wrote *Mrs Tim Gets a Job, Kate Hardy, Young Mrs Savage and Vittoria Cottage*. All these books were quite as successful as their predescessors and *Young Mrs Savage* was chosen by the American Family Reading Club as their Book of the Month. My new novel *Music in the Hills* is in the same genre and all those who have read it think it is one of my best. A businessman, who lives in London, wrote to me saying "*Music in the Hills* is as good as a holiday and, although I have read several other books since reading it, the peaceful atmosphere lingers in my mind. I hope your next book will tell us more about James and Rhoda and the other characters for they are so real to me and have become my friends." The scene of this book is laid in the hills and valleys of the Scottish Borders and the people are the rugged individualistic race who inhabit this beautiful country. For a long time it has been in my mind to write a story with this setting and to try to describe the atmosphere, to paint an artistically true picture of life in this district. Now it is finished and I hope my large and faithful public will enjoy reading it as much as I have enjoyed writing it.

Sometimes I have been accused of making my characters "too nice". I have been told that my stories are "too pleasant", but the fact is I write of people as I find them and am fond of my fellow human beings. Perhaps I have been fortunate but in all my wanderings I have met very few thoroughly unpleasant people, so I find it difficult to write about them.

We live in Moffat now. Moffat is a small but very interesting old town which lies in a valley between round

213

rolling hills. Some of the buildings are very old indeed but outside the town there are pleasant residential houses with gardens and fine trees of oak and beech and elm. From my window as I write I can see the lovely sweep of moorland where the small, lively, black-faced sheep live and move and have their being. Every day the hills look different: sometimes grey and cold, sometimes green and smiling; in winter they are often white with snow or hidden in soft grey mist, in September they are purple with heather, like a royal robe. Although Moffat is isolated there is plenty of society and many interesting people to talk to and entertain and it is only fifty miles from Edinburgh so, if I feel dull, I can go and stay there at my comfortable club and see a good play or a film and do some shopping.

There are several questions which recur again and again in letters from friends and acquaintances. Perhaps I should try to answer them. The first is, why do you write? I write because I enjoy writing more than anything. It is fascinating to think out a story and to feel it taking shape in my mind. Of course I like making money by my books —who would not?—but the money is a secondary consideration, a by-product as it were. The story is the thing. Writing a book is the most exciting adventure under the sun.

The second question is, how do you write? I write all my books in longhand, lying on a sofa near the window in my drawing room. I begin by thinking it all out and then I take a pencil and jot it all down in a notebook. When that stage is over I begin at the beginning and go on like mad until I get to the end. After that I have a little rest and then polish it up and rewrite bits of it. When I can do no more to it I pack it up, smother the parcel with sealing wax, and despatch it to be typed. I am now free as air and somewhat dazed, so I ring up all my friends (who have been neglected for months) and say, "Come and have a party."

Another question is, do you draw your characters from real life? The answer is definitely NO. The characters in a novel are the most interesting part of it and the most mysterious. They must come from Somewhere, I suppose, but they certainly do not come from "real life". They begin by taking shape in a nebulous form and then, as I think about them and live with them, they become more solid and individualistic with definite ideas of their own. Sometimes I get rather annoyed with them; they are so unmanegeable, they flatly refuse to do as I want and take their own way in an arbitrary fashion.

All the people in my books are real to me. They are more real than the people I meet every day for I know them better and understand them more deeply. It is difficult to say which is my favourite character, for I am fond of them all, but the most *extraordinary* character I ever had to deal with was Sophonisba Marks (in my novel *The Two Mrs. Abbotts.*) I intended her to be a subsidiary character, an unimportant person in the story, but Miss Marks had other ideas. In spite of the fact that she was plain and elderly and somewhat deaf and suffered severely from rheumatism, Miss Marks walked straight into the middle of the stage and stayed there. She just *wouldn't* take a back seat. She is so real to me that I simply cannot believe she does not exist. Somewhere or other she *must* exist—perhaps I shall meet her one day! Perhaps I shall see her in the street, coming towards me clad in her black cloth coat and the round toque with the white flowers in it and carrying her umbrella in her hand. I shall stop her and say loudly (because of course she is deaf) "Miss Marks, I presume!"

It will be seen from the foregoing sketch that my life has not been a very eventful one. I have had no hair-raising adventures nor travelled in little-known parts of the world, but wherever I have been I have made interesting friends and I still retain them. Friends are like windows in a house, and what a terribly dull house it would be that had no windows! They open vistas, they show one new and lovely views of the countryside. Friends give one new ideas, new values, new interests.

Thank God for friends!

Someday I mean to write a book of reminiscences; to delve into the cupboard of memory and sort out all the junk. There is so much to write about, so many little pictures grave and gay, so many ideas to think about and disentangle and arrange. Looking back is a fascinating pastime; looking back and wondering what one's life would have been if one had done this instead of that, if one had turned to the left at the crossroads instead of to the right, if one had stayed at home instead of going out or had gone out five minutes later. Jane Welsh Carlyle says in one of her letters, "One can never be too much alive to the consideration that one's every slightest action does not end when it has acted itself but propagates itself on and on, in one shape or another, through all time and away into eternity."

AN EXCITING ADVENTURE

D. E. Stevenson
talks about three of her novels

MUSIC IN THE HILLS

Why did I write *Music in the Hills?*

Although I have now written a score of novels it is still an exciting adventure to fare forth upon a new story and *Music in the Hills* was a particularly exciting adventure. For a long time I had been contemplating a story to be set in the hills of the Scottish Border country which I know and love so well; a story which, though fiction, should be artistically true so that other people all over the world in very different kinds of lands should be able to visualise the country and make friends with its inhabitants. It seems to me that this job of interpreting my own people to other people is the most important contribution I can make to the world and to peace.

How did it all begin?

All stories must have a pushing off place, a wharf from which the voyage starts, and *Music in the Hills* began with Mamie Johnstone. Mamie lived with me for months; she was a charming companion whose presence became more real daily. Gradually the other people congregated round her; the plot took shape; the river began to flow and the hills and valleys end farms settled into their appointed places. The locale of the story is not geographically correct but it is a composite picture of a river and hills in the Scottish Borders.

As the story unfolded Mureth stole my heart; I lived

there in spirit, I wandered over the hirsel with the shepherd Daniel Reid who had travelled far and wide and come home to Mureth; I helped James to drain the meadow and with him watched the golden moon rise from behind the hills and I sat in the drawing-room listening to Mamie's music. I was so enchanted with Mureth that when the story ended I could not say good-bye—so now I am writing another story about the same place and the same people. *Shoulder the Sky* is another exciting adventure.

What do my readers say?

My post-bag is full of letters from all over the world and the curious thing is that so many of these letters tell me that my books are a cure for loneliness. Perhaps this is because I open the door and invite my readers to come in, to sit down at the fire and take part in the life of my characters. So many of these letters ask the same question: are the characters real? They are not portraits of flesh and blood people but they are very real to me. They come from some unknown source and by thinking about them constantly I come to know them and share their joys and sorrows. They are not mere puppets and often refuse to walk in the path I have chosen for them—in this they are like one's friends who seldom take good advice.

How do I write my books?

All my books are written in longhand for the click of a typewriter is deadening to the imaginataion: a typewriter though extremely useful is not romantic. I write near the window in the drawing-room with the rolling hills of the Borders spread out before my eyes. Various members of the family come into the room and talk and go away again, sometimes they find me a little *distraite* and unable to concentrate upon important matters, but I do my best to help John to decide which of two attractive invitations he should accept, whether the fish should be fried or grilled and if this would be a good day to have a bonfire in the garden. Occasionally when my patience begins to wear thin I hang a notice upon the door, a notice which says "WRITING" in large letters, but even this does not bring me absolute peace.

Now for my method: the first stage is a collection of random jottings in a large notebook, then, when the plot and the characters and the location are all clear in my mind, I begin at the beginning and write like mad until I get to the end. After that most of it has to be rewritten for, like my cousin Robert Louis Stevenson I am a believer in working at a phrase until I have got it rounded and polished and shorn of unnecessary words. When I can do no more I pack up the manuscript securely, smother the parcel with sealing-wax and send it away to be typed . . . and now I am free as air, and somewhat dazed, so I ring up my friends who have been neglected for months and say, "Come and have a party!"

THE ROLE OF THE STORYTELLER

WHEN I HEARD THAT the Peoples Book Club had chosen *Shoulder the Sky* as their book for April, I felt very happy, for it meant they had enjoyed *Music in the Hills.*

Most love stories end with marriage bells, like *Music in the Hills*, but in real life marriage is not the end of the story. Marriage is not en easy relationship, and those who set forth upon married life in the belief that all will be smooth sailing are heading for disaster. The first wild rapture fades, and unless there is Something Else to take its place there is nothing left but two separate people tied together. Fortunately, most married people discover Something Else: loving kindness, loyalty and the sharing of joys and sorrows make them partners in the battle of life. In *Shoulder the Sky* James and Rhoda are forming this new and abiding relationship which is the mystery of marriage. But James and Rhoda are not the only people in *Shoulder the Sky,* and I must confess that some of the minor characters gave me a great deal of pleasure. How I enjoyed Mrs. Ogylvie Smith! She was so full of life that I could have written a whole book about her. I could have written much more about the Heddles—especially about Miss Heddle. Duggie was interesting and unusual and I have a feeling he is really the hero of *Shoulder the Sky,* for like the swineherd in the traditional fairy-tale, he started life poor and miserable and ended rich and happy.

The profession of the storyteller is a very ancient one. Before the dawn of history, when men lived in caves end wore the skins of beasts, the storyteller was a power in the land; he was a privileged member of his tribe and was always sure of a good seat near the fire when the day's hunting was over. We can imagine how his audience hung upon his words, their eyes fixed upon his face as he whiled away the long winter evenings with tales of hunting or of battle. This storyteller was first and foremost an entertainer—and well he knew it—for, if he failed to hold his audience entranced, all his precious privileges would he taken away from him and another more skilful spinner of tales would step into his shoes. That storyteller of old was the forbear of the modern novelist, and what was true in those far-off times is true today.

Some years ago I was talking to a literary club and in the course of my lecture I said that the first aim of a storyteller must be to entertain his audience. Some of the members disagreed; they thought it a paltry aim for a seriously-minded writer and declared that their aim was to elevate and instruct. But in spite of what those clever people said, it seems to me that if a storyteller does not succeed in entertaining his audience he will soon find himself telling his story to rows of empty seats—and to elevate and instruct empty seats is not much use to anybody. Besides, to offer entertainment need not he a paltry aim, for to entertain noble minds the entertainment must he of noble quality, full of truth and beauty.

Every age and clime has its own literature, the literature which suits its people and incidentally interprets them to others. The novel is particularly valuable as a medium of interpretation, for here we come into close contact with the mind of the author and see the world through his eyes. You see views of other countries and other people which enlarge our interests and, even better, enlarge our sympathies with our fellow human beings. A good novel about some other country gives us a much clearer idea of what that country is like than any travel book or guide book. Facts are cold and hard; they do not stir the imagination, and without the help of imagination we cannot see with the inward eye.

A novel is not true in fact, but the author must have the power of making it true to us; he must take us by the hand and bring us right inside the family circle. Most important of all, he must make us believe that his characters are real people of flesh and blood, so that we can identify ourselves with them, sharing their difficulties, struggling beside them through their adversities and rejoicing with them when finally they win happiness and peace.

FIVE WINDOWS

THE STORY ABOUT DAVID KIRKE, his mother and father and his friends, was in my mind for a long time before I put pen to paper. In a way it was an experiment for I wanted to put myself into the skin of a little boy and see the world through his eyes. A story told in the first person limits one's scope considerably, for nothing must go into the story except what the writer sees. Nothing must go into the story except what the writer feels. With David Kirke I ran about the hills and moors, and went to school. It all had to be told in very simple language. Then as he grew older and developed the outlook became more adult, the reactions more mature . . . but David was still a simple creature, the product of his sheltered upbringing. People have criticised David and have told me he was a sap—too good to be true. But he is not intended to he a "hero". And surely, even in this sophisticated world, there must still be Davids. Perhaps they feel a little bewildered when they adventure forth and meet with dragons. David did not know much about Life, he did not even know much about himself. All this was difficult at first but soon it became easier and my pen ran on happily to the end. I think it would be true to say that *Five Windows* gave me more pleasure to write than any of my other books.

THE AUTHOR'S POINT OF VIEW

Some notes for a talk to members of The Book Trade and other Businessmen and women in Glasgow. It was arranged by Messrs. Collins and given in their premises in Cathedral Street. They enjoyed the jokes but very few of them had any useful suggestions to offer, however Messrs. Collins seemed quite satisfied – and said there was a good deal of "useful talk" when I had come away!

THE AUTHOR'S POINT OF VIEW

WHEN Messrs Collins asked me to give this talk I felt greatly honoured. I have a done a good deal of speaking (to the P.E.N. Club, and to various other literary societies, to several Burns Clubs, to the English Speaking Union, to Church Guilds and Women's Institutes and to Robert Louis Stevenson Clubs) but I have never before spoken to a meeting of businessmen and women. Mr. Shakeshaft said I was to tell you how an author works—and about the problems of an author—and about the taste of the public. He said I was at liberty to criticise my publishers —so that sounds very nice!

You will realise that, under the circumstances, this talk is going to be all about *me* (on reading over my notes I was quite horrified to discover it was so egotistical) but I can't help that. If it absolutely unbearable you must blame Mr. Skakeshaft, and not me. I thought it would be a good plan to talk for about half an hour; then you can ask questions and offer any ideas that may occur to you.

First; how does an author work? This is difficult to answer because no two authors work in the same way. I can only tell you about novels (I know nothing about other forms of literature) and I can only tell you about my own method of writing and not about other novelists. I happen to know that some writers of fiction start at the beginning of their story and have no idea how it is going to finish—and sometimes they get all tied up and cannot find a way out of the tangle! Some authors type their

229

stories, others dictate them. These methods would not suit me. My method is to think about my story for months before I set pen to paper. So, when I begin to write, I know exactly where I am going and I can set out upon my expedition with confidence.

A book is very like an expedition and I am sure you will agree that if you were going to lead an expedition you would like to go over the ground beforehand and make yourself familiar with the route, so that, when you started, you and your company could set off together at a steady pace, making for a definite objective. There is no time lost, straying about.

The characters in my books are very important. I think about them for a long time and get to know them intimately. I know much more about them than what actually appears in the book – where they were born and how they were brought up—I know all their idiosyncrasies and their likes and dislikes—even minor characters in the story are carefully studied and drawn. Quite possibly none of these details about them are mentioned in the book but the details make the characters real to me—and therefore to my readers. I cannot overstress the importance of this. Obviously it makes the characters flesh and blood people—not puppies but human beings—and for this reason they capture the readers' heart.

There is one disadvantage of this: being real, they cannot act out of character to meet the requirements of the plot, but often insist upon going their own way. There was Miss Marks, for instance. She appeared in my novel *The Two Mrs. Abbotts;* and I intended her to be a minor character, but Miss Marks had such a forceful personality that she refused to stay minor! Miss Marks was plain and dumpy, she was very deaf and suffered from rheumatism but in spite of these disabilities she acted all the other characters off the stage and became, to all intents and purposes, the heroine of the story . . . incidentally she caught a German spy. I had intended young Mrs. Abbott to catch the spy of course, but Miss Marks did it herself, armed with her umbrella. Never, before or since, have I had to deal with such a refractory character. It was quite alarming.

But, enough of Miss Marks.

While I am "thinking out" my book I make copious notes and write out pieces of the story. Then, when it is all perfectly clear, I begin at the beginning and write the whole book in long-hand lying upon a large old-fashioned sofa in my sitting-room. The windows are large and there is a lovely view of meadows and trees and hills—rounded Lowland hills with sheep grazing peacefully—and clouds and sunshine in the ever-changing sky.

Meanwhile the affairs of daily life go on as before: my husband comes in to tell me that a hare has got into the garden and has eaten a whole row of seedling lettuces, or the slugs have got at his peas. My housekeeper comes in to ask if I remembered to order the fish for supper . . . and of course I have not remembered! It is too late now, the fish-van has passed—so what can be done? The problem seems insolvable until suddenly one of us conceives a brilliant idea. The little boy from the farm will be passing through the town on his way home from school, and usually calls at the stationer's for his father's evening paper, so all we have to do is to ring up and ask Mr. Haddock to send our fish over to him. Johnny will get a shilling for his trouble and everybody will be happy, so it is an admirable solution to the problem for everybody except me. For me it has wasted half an hour and has taken my mind completely off my work.

The next thing that happens to disturb me is the sound of children's voices in the garden. Children's voices are supposed to be delightful—but these are not, or at least not to me. I bear it for a bit and then I hear a loud splash and screams of distress and rush out to see if one of the little darlings has fallen into the burn. I discover several boys from a near-by school engaged in making a dam in the burn—and using stones from the rockery to reinforce their work. They have done this before with disastrous results—the burn overflowed and poured through our vegetable plot washing out several lines of french beans. They were *told* about this and warned not to do it again— yet here they are doing it again. When they see me coming they fly for their lives—a sure sign of guilt—and I am left to tidy up the mess after tea.

After this episode I am at liberty to return to work— and perhaps I have time to collect my thoughts and settle down and write half a page—when an old lady calls to ask for my subscription to the Society for the Prevention of Cruelty to Children. "I won't interrupt you," she declares, "but I happened to be passing and I just thought—I mean, you gave ten shillings last year—so . . ." I fell inclined to tell her that she *has* interrupted me and that I am in no mood to subscribe to the object, but I stifle this impulse and fork out ten shillings and see her off at the door. No sooner has she gone then the joiner arrives to "sort" the roof of the tool-shed.

These things don't happen every day of course, or my books would never get written at all. Some days I get quite a lot of peace, and I must admit that once I get going on the final draft of my story I become deaf and blind to the outside world: children can flood the garden, hares can eat the lettuces and old ladies call in vain for subscriptions to the R.S.P.C.C. I get up early and write before breakfast and, except for meals, I continue to write until late at night.

To begin with an author must have a story to tell— something that bubbles up inside and demands expression. But he must also have the means of expression—in other words, technique. How does he learn?

There are schools of painting and schools of music but an author must find his own way amongst the shoals. I started writing stories when I was eight years old. My parents were not encouraging and I was obliged to find a place to hide when the urge to write was upon me. I made a nest in the box-room between two large solid leather trunks. There was an old brown blanket to sit on and a skylight overhead so it really was an exceedingly good study, peaceful and comfortable. I still have some of the stories I wrote when I was a child—they are very bad and not in the least funny. I was no Daisy Ashford who wrote a best-seller (*The Young Visiters*) when she was nine years old.

Their Black Leader was my most ambitious effort. It is about a little black girl who found a part of grown-up people lost in the jungle and led them to safety. All manner of adventures befell them, adventures with lions and tigers and crocodiles, encounters with cannibals. There was a forest fire and a flooded river . . . Obviously I had been studying Henty and Fennimore Cooper when I wrote the story, and there is a dash of *Swiss Family Robinson* and Jules Verne about it as well.

The only interesting point about this is that it shows so very clearly the influence of *reading* on the young mind . . . and it seems to me that the modern child's diet of comics is a very poor substitute for Fennimore Cooper, Henty and Jules Verne!

From my earliest days I *was* a voracious reader of every sort of book that came my way. Then, as I grew older and decided to make writing my career, I began to study the subject with care. I took stories to pieces and tried to find out how they were made. Why was *this* book so interesting and so easy to read that one could not put it down? Why was *that* book so dull? Why was this book memorable and that one forgotten in a night?

It would take too long to tell you how I read and studied and wrote and learnt my trade. You see, it is not enough to have a story to tell, you must learn the best way to tell it. I learnt by trial and error, which I believe is the only way to success as a writer.

Perhaps you will smile when I mention the great French novelist, Flaubert, in connection with my own, admittedly light, novels, but I learnt one very important lesson from him. In his novel, *Madame Bovary,* everything that happens is seen through Madame Bovary's eyes—and yet, in spite of this, we become aware of many things which Madame Bovary did not see. This is what

234

makes the book so fascinating and so interesting to the student of literature—and also makes the book easy to read. The spotlight is focussed upon one character all the time; it does not flick about first on one character and then on another.

Of course you can obtain much the same result from writing the story in the first person—my cousin, R.L.S. was very fond of this method of presentation—but there are various snags here, as every author knows.

Since reading *Madame Bovary*, which was more years ago than I can remember, I have practised the method of seeing and hearing through the eyes and ears of a single character. All the other characters in the story are seen in this way. Their peculiarities are revealed by what they say and do. The reader is not told what they are thinking and feeling.

Perhaps you will think this method of concentrating the spotlight upon a single character is unnecessarily restricting to the unfolding of the plot but I am convinced that it enhances the interest and makes the story easier to read. Quite recently I read a novel by a well-known author. The spotlight was turned this way and that—we were told what A was thinking and what B felt about the matter, we were given C's point of view. It was a good story and well written But I found it difficult to read. I found it rather muddling.

In my novel *Still Glides the Stream* the first part of the story is seen through the eyes of Will Hastie and the second part through the eyes of Patience Elliot Murray. None of my readers will realise this, of course—or at least very few—but I am certain that all my readers will

235

appreciate the *effect* and find the book easy to read. I have used the same method in several other books: in *Spring Magic* and in *Katharine's Marriage* for instance; but, as a general rule, the spotlight is concentrated upon a single character from beginning to end. It is either written in the first person, like *Five Windows*, *Katharine Wentworth* and *Sarah Morris Remembers* or else it is written entirely from one person's point of view.

So far I have said nothing about style, but style is very important to me and sometimes I spend hours re-writing passages. Quite often I read them aloud to make sure that they satisfy my ear . . . but, even when I am engaged upon this task, I have an uneasy suspicion that I'm wasting my time. How many of my readers will appreciate the results of my labour? Some will, of course, and perhaps others will enjoy the feeling of running along smoothly, as they would enjoy the easy riding of a well-sprung motor car, but really it is for my own pleasure that I bother about style. There is a rhythm in prose that enchants me and it pleases me enormously to find exactly the right word and to put it in exactly the right place.

We come now to the taste of the public. How are we to gauge this? I'm afraid I don't bother about it much. I write to please myself, and if other people are pleased so much the better. Reviewers used to help a good deal when I began to write, but reviewing seems to be a lost art; a résumé of the plot is the modern idea—all the secrets are given away with scarcely any comment. Fan mail doesn't help much either for, although I get hundreds of letters, these correspondents are only a very small proportion of the thousands who read my books—

and nearly all the letters are from people who *like* my boooks. This is natural of course, for very few people who *dislike* a book would bother to write to the author—they would throw it down with a groan or return it to the library and make a note not to get any more rubbish by the same author! Letters come from all over the world, and I answer them all. They come from Bournemouth and Inverness and Cardiff and Greenock, from South Carolina and Massachusetts, from California, Boston and Chicago, from Cape Town and Johannesburg, Melbourne and Calcutta and Hong Kong. Most of the people who write to me want more about characters who have become their friends—more about James and Rhoda, more about Katharine Wentworth, more about Mrs. Tim—or they want to know where they can get some of my older books which have gone out of print. Not long ago I had a letter from a young man in an oil company in Iraq. His name is Roger Ayrton and he asked if I would be so kind as to put him in touch with the Ayrtons of Amberwell. He was sure they must be his relations. He was coming home on leave quite soon and would it be all right if he dropped in at Amberwell to see them? I was obliged to write back and confess that there was no such place as Amberwell and no such family as the Ayrtons. They were all imaginary. I said I was sorry I had borrowed his name—Roger Ayrton—and bestowed it upon my hero, but it was no more than a curious coincidence. Now he has written saying he has read the book again and he can't believe that the people are imaginary . . . they are real people, flesh and blood people, and have become his friends. He added that he was very disappointed; he has no near relations and was looking forward to meeting Roger and Nell and Anne. It is rather a sad letter and has made me feel quite guilty.

Fan mail is interesting in various ways. As I said before, the letters come from all over the world, and, even more interesting, they come from all sorts and conditions of people. Lately, and by the same post, I got two letters: one from an elderly professor of history at Oxford and the other from a charwoman who lives in a Glasgow tenement. The latter apologised for her spelling and not without reason!

If these two individuals met they would have nothing in common, they would scarcely understand each other's language, yet both had enjoyed the same book, and, when I had read their letters carefully, I found they had like the book for the same reason (of course their reasons were expressed in different words but they *meant* the same thing). The charwoman said it seemed so real that she felt she was *there.* It was like having a holiday, she said. And the people were so nice that she was sorry when she got to the end.

The professor explained that he did not read novels—as a general rule. His subject was history. His search was for truth. But his wife had given him my book to read when he was in bed with a cold and he had enjoyed in immensely. He said various nice things about it including the statement that it was a complete whole and its end was implicit in its beginning. He said it had the inevitability of a Great Drama, and, like a Great Drama, it embodied Truth in Fiction.

I was pleased. Truth in Fiction is a fetish with me. I have given several talks on the subject to literary societies. I could talk about it for hours but it is not subject today so it is no use embarking on Truth in Fiction. A parable is not true in fact. A parable is a fictitious story told to illustrate a truth.

Perhaps it will amuse you to hear some of the things people say to an author and some of the things that happen which make writing stories such a delightful occupation.

One day I went to lunch with a friend of mine and when we had finished our exceedingly good meal, my friend asked if I would mind coming into the kitchen and meeting her cook who enjoyed reading my books. The cook was an elderly Scotswoman with sparse grey hair and bright blue eyes. She gazed at me in a slightly disappointed manner. "You don't look like an author," she said. I said I was sorry—what else could I say? "Oh well," said the cook. "It's nice to see you anyway. I've wasted an awful lot of time reading your stories." My friend was horrified—but as a matter of fact I thought it was a very nice compliment and was suitable gratified.

Then there are the people who say, "What a nice hobby!" or "What an easy was to make money!" or, confidentially, "You know, I'm sure I could write a novel if only I had time."

I think I've told you enough to show you that writing a book isn't very easy—there is a lot of hard work in it. I have told you enough to show you that I take it very seriously indeed; in addition to this I feel that writing a book, which is going to be read by thousands and thousands of people all over the world and translated into Dutch and German and Danish, and other European languages—is a big responsibility. I like to think that nobody is any the worse for reading my books—and some people are better and happier.

Everybody is not happier of course. For instance there was the woman who came up to me at a big Charity Bazaar which I had just opened, with suitable remarks. "I'm Lizzie," said the woman truculently.

"You're Lizzie?" I echoed in bewildered accents—I had never seen her before! "I'm Lizzie," she repeated. "You wrote all about me in yon book about Mureth Farm. All about how I'd been evacuated from Glasgow with the two children. Och, you changed the names of course, but it was me just the same."

I was speechless—for the woman called Lizzie in *Winter and Rough Weather* was by no means an admirable character. She was sly and deceitful, and exceedingly stupid—in fact was practically moronic! (Of course I have met other people who identified themselves with characters in my books, but they always chose a pleasing sort of character—most of us see ourselves in a favourable light.)

"Well, what have you got to say?" enquired the woman at the Charity Bazaar. "Where did you hear about me? Who told you about me?"

I did my best to explain that "Lizzie", as depicted in my book, was an imaginary person.

"Maybe it was Jean MacLaggan told you?" suggested the woman suspiciously.

"It was nobody," I declared. "I never heard of you, nor Jean MacLaggan either. The Lizzie in my book isn't a real person."

She didn't believe me. She went off, muttering under her breath. "The cheek of it!" I heard her say. "The cheek of it—to put me in a book! Me and the children!"

I couldn't help laughing; it was so ridiculous. Perhaps she really was Lizzie—my imaginary Lizzie—come to life!

But now we must be serious.

Some time ago there was an article in a literary journal which interested me greatly. The article was by a well-known literary critic, Kenneth Allsop, and was entitled "No Time for Reading". This is what he said: "Why don't people read more? Do they hate or fear books? Do they even know there *are* books? So far as I know the publishing trade has made no serious attempt to find the answer to these questions."

Mr. Allsop went out and made enquiries from various people he met in the street and out of thirty people he questioned only one liked books and bought them regularly. Some of the people said they had no time to read, others said they preferred T.V., others explained that books were too expensive.

I can't altogether agree with Mr. Allsop's findings, for the people he questioned were all *the same kind of people* and I doubt whether they had ever been Buyers of Books or ever would be. For one thing they referred to books as "stiff-covered books" —which was rather a give-away!— but I suppose there must be something in Mr. Allsop's contention and, if there is a grain of truth in it, the Book

Trade might do well to consider the matter and find the answer.

I have thought of several possible reasons why people don't read more. I suggest them for your consideration:

1.   Are people illiterate? I mean are there people who find reading so laborious that there is no pleasure in it? Either because they have never *learnt* to read easily or because they have forgotten all they learnt at school? I know this sounds almost impossible in these days of free education, but I have reason to believe that quite a lot of people are, to all intents and purposes, illiterate.

2.   Is it because there are too many newspapers and magazines and too much television, so that people have got into the habit of getting snippets presented to them on a plate without having to bother to use their brains?

3.   Is it restlessness? Restlessness is a modern disease. People can't settle down comfortably with their feet in the fender and enjoy reading a book.

4.   Does the fault lie in the books which are offered to the public?

I know I am on thin ice here, but I'm going to risk it! I think you will agree that many modern novels are extremely depressing. Do people really enjoy being depressed? Do they *like* reading about depraved characters with cruel and unnatural habits? They wouldn't want to meet horrible characters in real life so why should they want to meet them in a book? Why should they be willing to pay a guinea—or more—for the privilege of meeting disagreeable people and being made unhappy? Perhaps one of these suggestions may be the answer to Mr. Allsop's question: "Why don't people read more?"

Fortunately for me this problem does not arise, for I have my own satisfied circle of readers who buy my books or borrow them from libraries—or steal them from their friends! Sometime ago, when I saw Mr. Collins, the chairman of the firm, he told me that the sales of fiction had gone down, adding with a smile, "Except, of course, you and Agatha."

I was amused, but afterwards I thought about it seriously. Agatha Christie is very special, of course. She is a genius in her own line. I buy every book she writes and enjoy them enormously. My case is different and more difficult to understand but if I had to give a reason for the popularity of my books (the sales to date in Britain and America are over four million) I am inclined too think that the old Glasgow charwoman put it in a nutshell: she felt she was *there;* it was like having a holiday—and the people were so nice that she was sorry when she got to the end.

Now we come to the last item on my list. I have been told to criticize my publishers! Messrs. Collins have published my books for over thirty years and all that time they have been very kind to me. We have never had a shadow of disagreement—except about jackets! It seems to me that jackets are very important indeed—and it seems to me that the designers of jackets show a lack of initiative, a lack of punch. How few jackets are arresting to the eye! How few give one any idea of the contents of the book!

In my novel, *Young Mrs. Savage,* I stressed the point that young Mrs. Savage had golden curls and blue eyes. I mentioned the fact half a dozen times in the course of the story; it was essential to the plot that the lady should be so endowed. Imagine my feelings when I saw the cover of the Fontana edition of the book which depicted a gypsy girl with long black straggly hair lounging on the beach! It was a shock to other people too, and I received numerous letters from irate readers asking why Mrs. Savage had dyed her hair. I was so cross that I put the letters into an envelope and forwarded them to Messrs. Collins. As usual Messrs. Collins were polite and tactful; they assured me that the book was selling like hot cakes— a statement calculated to sooth the feelings of any but the most refractory author.

Ever since that unfortunate occurrence Messrs. Collins make a point of sending me the artist's proof for my approval. I can imagine them saying, "For God's sake send that woman the artist's design! You know what an awful fuss she makes about her jackets!"

Perhaps they don't say this—but I expect they *do.* Anyhow, they send it. Sometimes I approve and sometimes not.

In *The Tall Stranger* my hero and heroine met for the first time at a very smart wedding; the reception took place in a garden and I described how my hero came out of the large marquee bearing a tray upon which there was a slab of wedding-cake and two glasses of champagne.

The artist's design was sent for my approval—and what was my surprise to see a young man emerging from a small tent with two cups of tea, one in each hand! What was my horror to notice that, at this *very* smart wedding, the gentleman guests had seen fit to turn up in grey slacks, tweed jackets and open-necked shirts! These details were altered at my request—but should the mistake have occurred? *Would* the mistake have occurred if the artist had read the typescript of the novel, sent especially for his perusal?

In America the case is rather different. Mr. John O'Hara Cosgrave has designed the jackets for my books, and designed them beautifully, for years. But even he slipped up on one occasion, when he designed the jacket for *Music in the Hills.* In this particular story it is essential to the plot that two farms, one on each side of the river, have no means of communication with each other save by a ford—and this ford is impassable when the river rises. Evidently Mr. Cosgrave was of the opinion that this was inconvenient for he depicted a bridge across the river and a horse and cart crossing the bridge in comfort! The design was attractive and the book sold well so it didn't matter very much—except that I received sheaves of letters pointing out "the mistake" and was obliged to answer them.

Perhaps you will think I am too fussy? But it seems strange to me that publishers should not take more interest in packaging their wares. Packaging is important —more important nowadays that ever before. Look around a grocer's shop and notice the attractive packaging of breakfast cereals and cake-mixtures and all the other comestibles! Notice the different packets of soap-powder with gay pictures on them! The makers will tell you that it pays to advertise and that an attractive picture on the packet helps to sell the goods.

What about books? Does an attractive jacket help to sell a book? Many members of my audience are booksellers so perhaps they can answer this question.

In my opinion two things are necessary in a jacket: an attractive and arresting design, and a design that will show what sort of matter the book contains. Both are equally important.

I have tried to give you an author's point of view and I hope you may find it useful. After all, you must admit that an author is quite an important person in the Book Trade; for without authors there would be no books—and therefore no Book Trade.

THE PERFECT MURDER

THE PERFECT MURDER
A Detective Story

In most detective stories, and I suppose in real life, the murderer is discovered because the body is discovered and because the victim has disappeared from his usual haunts. The disappearance of the victim and the discovery of his body are linked together and provide a basis from which the detective starts to work. But if the body were to be discovered before the victim disappeared it would make things a good deal more difficult for the sleuth.

Impossible? Not really, if the murderer is clever. Here is the idea. Murdstone is a good name for the murderer—and we can call the victim Vance. It starts with a V and so does victim. We have no time for details so you can fill those in for yourself. We start straight off by saying that for some reason Murdstone had decided that the world will be more comfortable for him if Vance moves on to the next. The two men both live in a small town in Sussex. They both have wives and families—this makes it more difficult of course. They both go up to London every day to business, usually by train, but Murdstone sometimes drives to work in his car. Murdstone hears that Vance is going to London on Monday for a business meeting on Tuesday, and will be staying there for a few days. He offers Vance a lift in his car and Vance accepts. Murdstone calls for Vance in his car and off they go. On the way they stop at a disused quarry and Murdstone kills Vance by hitting him on the head with a blunt instrument (the starting handle, perhaps). Murdstone takes off all Vance's clothes and packs them into a spare suitcase. He then batters Vance's face until it is not recognisable. Sorry about this brutality but it is necessary and after all murderers and victims in detective stories are never real. Murdstone drives on. When he gets to the next town he posts a postcard (which he has already prepared). It is addressed to the local police and printed upon it is the message "THERE IS A DEAD BODY IN WHINTON QUARRY." You see, he wants the body to be discovered at once. The police may think it is a hoax but they are bound to investigate.

Murdstone drives on to London. He arrives about five o'clock and goes to his hotel, where he has taken a room. His luggage is taken up. He talks to the porter, saying he is going out to dinner and the theatre and may be back pretty late. He thought of seeing a play called "Kingdom Come." "Very good play," replies the porter. Murdstone gives the porter half a crown and they talk about the play. In reality Murdstone has already seen this play but he pretends he has not.

Vance's luggage is still in the car. Murdstone goes out to the car and drives to a station. He goes to the Gentleman's toilet and there he changes into Vance's clothes. He also makes up to look like Vance. Vance wore spectacles and Murdstone has provided himself with a pair with plain glass. Vance was an outdoor man and had a tanned skin—a little greasepaint does the trick. Fortunately Vance's clothes (a grey tweed suit and a soft hat) fit Murdstone none too badly. This is the only bit of luck he has. Murdstone is much too clever to trust to

250

luck; he prefers to trust his brains and to have his plans cut and dried.

Murdstone then drives to another hotel, asks for a room and gives his name as Vance. He gets the page to send off a wire to Vance's wife, saying "Decided to stay at the Majestic. Please forward letters. Back on Friday if all goes well—Harry." Murdstone then goes and has dinner. He sits in the lounge. He talks to the porter and tells him he is not feeling very well. He goes upstairs to his room, rings for a hot water bottle and when the chambermaid comes he is in bed. He tells her not to call him in the morning—he will ring when he wakes. He says he has a headache and is taking a couple of aspirins. She gives him the hot water bottle and goes away.

Immediately Murdstone gets up and dresses in his own clothes. He washes off the make-up and discards the spectacles. He is careful to wear gloves all the time he is in the room because of fingerprints. He puts Vance's clothes, which he has been wearing, in his suitcase, opens the door and seeing no sign of anyone he runs downstairs and into the street. He finds his car and drives to a garage, where he leaves his car and walks to the theatre. As he gets near to the theatre he gets out his pocket book—a nice one with his initials on it. He takes out the notes and puts them in his inside pocket. He drops the pocket book in the gutter. When he reaches the theatre the people are just coming out. Murdstone mixes with the crowd, then he pushes through them, back to the auditorium where the programme girls are already at work tipping up the seats and clearing up the place.

He gets hold of one of them and says he has lost his

pocket book. "I was sitting just here," he says. "You remember me, don't you? I bought a programme from you." He shows her the programme (he has picked it up on the stairs) and gives her half a crown. She likes him— he is such a nice gentleman and how awful for him to lose his money like that!—and she very easily persuades herself that she remembers him. They hunt about together. The manager arrives on the scene and the girl tells him about it: The gentleman was sitting just here— there's no sign of the pocket book—it must have been stolen. The manager is very distressed. He calls the police and a sergeant comes and takes down statements. By this time the girl is prepared to swear that she saw the gentleman sitting there, in the fifth row of the stalls; there is no doubt at all in her mind.

When the excitement is over the manager calls a tazi for Mr. Murdstone and he drives back to the hotel. The porter is very sympathetic about the pocket book— Murdstone tells him the whole story—then Murdstone goes up to bed. He lies in bed thinking about his day. Yes, he has remembered everything and carried out his plans without a hitch. The only thing left to do is to get rid of Vance's clothes (which are in the suitcase in the car). He decides to send the clothes to a firm of cleaners giving an assumed name and address—an excellent way of getting rid of them.

The next day the police find Murdstone's pocket book, empty of course, and it is returned to him. He thanks the police and says it cannot be helped, just what was to be expected, he is very glad to have the pocket book back, anyhow.

Vance is not missed until the afternoon, when he does not turn up at the meeting. His business friends telephone to his home and are told by his wife that Vance is staying at the Majestic. They send round to the hotel to find out about him; when his door is opened the room is found to be empty. Vance has vanished. What has become of him? Nobody knows. He was last seen by the chambermaid. She says he was in bed not feeling well, taking aspirins. The porter agrees—yes, he wasn't feeling well; he went up to bed early. The police ask for a description of Mr. Vance and are told that he had spectacles, rather a brown face, was wearing a grey tweed suit and a soft hat, Several other people saw Mr. Vance. The waiter remembers him at dinner: brown face he had, and glasses, grey tweed suit. The description is vague but the police are used to that for very few people can use their eyes or are able to give a proper description of a person. Besides, the police have no reason to suspect that the man was not Vance.

What can have become of Vance, that's the question. He may have lost his memory and be wandering about the country. He may have disappeared of his own accord. He may have been murdered, but if so where is his body? The police are completely mystified; there are no clues. The body in the quarry in Sussex cannot be the body of Vance. The idea that it might be never crosses their minds—*that* body was discovered on Monday evening by the local police and had already been dead some hours when Vance was eating his dinner at the Majestic Hotel. Murdstone is questioned of course, but no suspicion falls upon himand if it does he has a perfectly good alibi. The whole affair is an unsolvable mystery. The police make up their minds that Vance has done a bunk (no body, no murder) and Murdstone sits back comfortably. He has committed the perfect crime.

If I were going to write this story (which Heaven forbid) I might write it in this way, perfectly straightforward, from the murderer's point of view. I might write it in the first person, taking Murdstone himself as my storyteller. Murdstone delighted with himself, with his own cleverness, gloating over the deed. Then, when the deed is done and safely done, I might bring a detective on the scene, and I might pick flaws in the murder and bring it home to Murdstone. I think he would decide to kill himself and so cheat the hangman. Or again, I might start with the detective: the whole thing is wrapped in mystery and the detective—call him Dobbie—has to unravel it. Personally I would choose the first way, for what a splendid psychological study Murdstone would be! Murdstone seen from the inside, as he sees himself; Murdstone watching Dobbie at work; Murdstone laughing in his sleeve—and then beginning to be afraid as he sees Dobbie ferreting out the truth; Murdstone realising that Dobbie has a clue, a real clue, and that it is only a matter of time before the whole mystery will be solved; Murdstone deciding to put an end to himself.

But how could Dobbie solve the mystery? There are no loose ends; Murdstone has been too clever. Perhaps he is just a bit *too clever,* just a bit too pleased with himself, perhaps he underestimates Dobbie. Something he says to Dobbie rouses an odd sort of suspicion in Dobbie's mind, and Dobbie begins to poke about into Murdstone's past and finds that he had a motive for wanting Vance out of the way. He had a motive, says Dobbie to himself, but he had no opportunity. His alibi is watertight. For a bit Dobbie is stuck – and then some little fact comes to light and Dobbie gets a glimpse of the truth. It is odd, for instance, that nothing in the hotel bedroom, which Vance was supposed to have occupied, bears a trace of his fingerprints. His fingerprints are on his hair-brushes, and on all his personal effects, but there are no fingerprints ono the door of his wardrobe, nor anywhere else in the room. That's odd. It sets Dobbie thinking. Is it possible that Vance did not arrive safely in London? Gradually Dobbie collects evidence. He follows the course of the car in which Murdstone and Vance were supposed to have come to London. A policeman on point duty remembers his car. He is sure there was only one man in it. *Now* Dobbie is on the scent. He remembers the case of the unknown body which was found in Whinston Quarry and obtains permission for it to be exhumed. The face is unrecognisable but it is identified as Vance from the hair which is exactly the same as the hairs in Vance's hairbrush. The exhumation has been kept secret but Murdstone is following Dobbie's movements carefully. Murdstone is actually present in the churchyard, lurking behind a tombstone. He realises what is happening and his fear and despair get the upper hand. He realises that nothing can save him and rushing away he shoots himself.

So it is not the perfect murder after all.

TRUTH IN FICTION

*A talk given to the Soroptimists' Club
Edinburgh, 1946.*

TRUTH IN FICTION

WHEN I CHOSE this title I intended no epigram, nor do I mean to speak of authors who are said to borrow from real life for their material and whose borrowing may involve them in libel actions. I intend to speak quite straightforwardly about a different aspect of truth—artistic truth which is to be found in all good work.

Truth has a different meaning for different people and even the dictionary (a somewhat soulless guide to the meaning of words) admits this fact. The dictionary tells us that "truth in law is according to facts" but that "truth in art is a faithful adherence to nature." It is with the second truth, "the faithful adherence to nature" with which the novelist is concerned and with which I propose we should concern ourselves today.

Everybody who makes things with his head or his hands is looking for truth—striving for truth—for he is aware that beauty and worth must be based on truth. The lawyer seeks truth in the law court, the doctor seeks truth in diagnosing his cases, the architect seeks truth in design, the builder lays one stone upon another and sees to it that his lines are true.

You may think that a novelist is the last person to seek for truth, but in reality he seeks for it no less diligently than any of the other people I have mentioned: he seeks for his own particular brand of truth—faithfulness to nature—for unless a novel has this kind of truth inherent in its very bones, it is nothing more than a fairy-tale or a puppet show.

Many people enjoy fairy tales and puppet shoes but they cannot believe in them. We can only believe in people who are human like ourselves, not fairy princesses or dolls. We can only believe in events which we know might occur in real life, not the slaughter of dragons, and so it is that a novel must be like life if we are to enter into it and give our sympathy to its characters.

If a novelist is to entertain his fellow-men, if he is to excite their imagination and make them see things with his eyes, if he is to establish any sort of communication between his brain and theirs, his work must be alive: this quality can be found in all great novels and is really our old friend "truth", faithful adherence to nature.

There are many ways in which a novel must adhere to nature, and it is a little difficult to separate them for they all merge into one another, and indeed, unless they *do* so merge they are less than truth. I have divided them in a purely arbitrary manner under two headings, Scene and Characters. By "Scene" I mean the geographical environment in which the action of the novel takes place.

The author of a novel has two courses open to him: he can either take a real place, and plant his novel firmly in the soil of it, or he can manufacture a place of his own. For instance when Robert Louis Stevenson wrote *Kidnapped* he took a real place, well known to him, and planted his novel in the Highlands of Scotland. But when the same author wrote *Treasure Island* he made the island himself. In the first instance he set forth with an ash plant stick in his hand and tramped all over the hills where David Balfour wandered with Alan Breck. In the second instance he sat at home in his study and made Treasure Island out of his head.

There is much to be said for or against each of these courses. Many people think that a novel whose scene is laid in a real place gains at once and without extraneous aid, the verisimilitude of life, and this is true, for if we hear of a character wandering in a particular spot where we have wandered ourselves we have more reason for believing that he is flesh and blood like ourselves. That watchful critic who inhabits our brains and tells us in no uncertain voice: "Believe this," "Disbelieve that," is put off his guard when he sees such names as Edinburgh, Glasgow, London or North Berwick staring at him from the printed page. "Bless my soul!" he exclaims. "It's a real place!" And he gives us leave to believe in it—and in the characters walking about in it—if we can.

But this advantage is really not so important as it looks and it is outweighed in my opinion by certain disadvantages. And now I hope you will forgive me if I draw from my own experience to illustrate my point.

Personally I prefer the course which Robert Louis Stevenson took when he wrote *Treasure Island.* I prefer to make my own places out of my own head, and I prefer it for two reasons. First of all I am perfectly free, I can make a hill where I like, and I can make towns and villages exactly where I want them. There is no danger of some careful reader pouncing upon me and pointing out that a certain road does not run west and that therefore my hero could not have enjoyed looking at the sunset when he was walking along this road unless he had eyes

261

in the back of his head. Or another reader declaring that my heroine could not walk from one point to another in the given length of time unless she possessed a pair of seven league boots.

The second reason is very simple indeed: it is more fun to make your own place.

I have made quite a number of places, but Ardfalloch gave me more pleasure than all the others put together. I took a sea loch and surrounded it with mountains and pine forests. I had a salmon river of course, and a duck bog. I made a pass through the mountains too. I had moors just where I wanted them and roads and villages. I made a map of the whole thing—it was tremendous fun. When I had finished making it I was so in love with Ardfalloch that I wanted to go and live there.

The odd thing was that I had letters from people all over Scotland saying that they recognised their own district, from places so far apart as Ross and Argyll. A woman wrote to me from Australia and told me that she had left her home in Scotland when she was twelve years old, but that she recognised it at once, and would I tell her if old Mrs. Macfarlane was still alive, and was Alex still farming his croft, and was he married yet. Another woman wrote from America saying that she had always been interested in Scotland because her mother came from there and she added, "I have read all that I could get hold of about Scotland and now I feel I have seen it—I feel I have been to Ardfalloch myself."

I have said that characters in a novel must be *human beings* because if they are not we cannot interest ourselves in their fate. It is time, of course, that there are certain excellent detective stories in which the whole interest lies in the puzzle, or plot, and the characters are unimportant. They are really only puppets and the reader is not intended to interest himself in their personalities. These puppets are shot or poisoned, or done away with in some other ingenious manner, and the reader does not care. He does not drop a single tear upon their corpses, he is fully aware that they have no other *use* than to be shot or poisoned; they were created for that purpose.

But I am not concerned with detective stories today. I am concerned with novels in which the characters are *all-important,* with novels in which the play of personality is the underlying principle, and here once more we find truth essential. We *must* believe that the characters in a novel are real people (even though the author has solemnly assured us on the front page that they are not). We must believe in our hearts they are flesh and blood so that we may identify ourselves with them, and travel with them every step of their way, sharing their troubles and their sorrows, struggling beside them through misunderstandings and adventures and rejoicing with them wholeheartedly over the ultimate victory which usually attends their efforts. It is obvious that no characters could hold our interest from the first page to the last if they were made of sawdust. So much for the reader's point of view.

From the author's point of view the characters in his novel are extremely mysterious beings. He has no idea where they come from, not the slightest. They must come from somewhere I suppose, but it is very certain that they are not drawn from life. Characters in fiction are the most

263

unruly element with which a novelist has to deal – they sometimes bolt with the unfortunate author like a runaway horse. They are perfectly real, I assure you. They spring into life fully fledged and the author can not more alter their shape or squeeze them into a different mould that I could alter the shape of this glass without smashing it to atoms.

For instance, in a book I wrote called *The Two Mrs. Abbotts* there is an elderly lady called Miss Marks. She started by being quite an unimportant character, but halfway through she simply took the centre of the stage. She was more alive than anyone else in the book; her personality dominated the whole thing. She acted everybody else off the stage—and it was all done in the nicest way so that I really couldn't be angry with the woman. Miss Marks was elderly, she was stout and very deaf and a sufferer from rheumatism but in spite of these afflictions the indomitable woman refused to be coerced. I just had to let her do what she liked and make the best of it.

This personality—the colour or flavour of a person—can be imparted in various ways and perceived in various mediums.

We all know the feeling which assails us when we enter a house for the first time. There is a new smell about it, and a sort of sixth sense tells us immediately what this house is like, and what sort of people live in it. We say to ourselves, "This is a happy house, I should like to live here," or "This is a peaceful house, I should sleep well here," or again "There is something *not quite right* about this house—it is full of discord."

The houses which raise feelings of this nature in our breasts are sometimes old, historic buildings where terrible deeds of cruelty or bloodshed have been enacted, but sometimes they are quite ordinary modern houses which are inhabited by a strong personality, a personality strong in good or evil, and this personality has filled the atmosphere of the house with its flavour so that the very walls, the very fabric of the building is impregnated with that flavour.

I have said that an author does not draw his characters straight from real life and there are two reasons for this. One is that he does not need to. (They come to him, as I have already said, form some unknown source) and the other reason is even more strange. The characters is a novel must be *more real* than a real person. They must be *more like life* than you or I.

Perhaps you will think this quite absurd—how can a character be more life-like that a real person? And this atmosphere which can fill a house, and make it a good or an evil place to live in, can fill a book in the same way.

There are books which are apparently innocent, and are yet full of an atmosphere which is immoral and loose. There are books which are redolent of goodness and purity and peace—for instance the books of Louisa Alcott —and books which exude violence, tragedy and sin, such as *Wuthering Heights.*

And so we come to atmosphere, the most difficult to explain, the most difficult to achieve. What do we mean when we speak of the atmosphere of a novel? I think we mean the tinge of colour which the author imparts to all that he describes—the tinge of colour which is really the author's self, his own personality. This personality, the colour or the flavour of a person, can be communicated in various ways and perceived in various mediums. The air which surrounds the characters in a novel must be the atmosphere of this world in which we live.

This is the purpose of a novel, this is its function. It is thus that it justifies its existence in the fabric of society. We come into contact with the mind of its author, we are taken into close communion with another soul. Novels are like windows looking out onto different views—views of history, views of other countries, and, no less valuable, unfamiliar views of our own country and of the people who inhabit our own land. Novels enlarge our interests, enlarge our minds, and best of all they enlarge our sympathies with our fellow men and women.

There are many novels which do none of these things of course: they should never have been written and should most certainly never be read!

We see therefore that the scene the characters and the atmosphere of a novel must be not merely true to life, but *living*. And so we come to the Theme, which knits them all into one living whole. From the theme the novel grows, and it develops within the limits of the theme, so that unless the theme of the novel is full of truth and beauty, the whole work is a waste of time.

The scene, the characters and the atmosphere must all merge into one theme, and the theme must be part of the Spirit of Truth.

Or, to put it differently, there must be some definite idea, some profound thought, some thread which strings the whole thing together and gives it meaning, gives it coherence and point, and this underlying theme must be a facet of truth, just as a parable is a facet of truth.

Any great novel, or indeed any novel that is worth reading, is really a parable. It describes fictitious places, fictitious people and fictitious events to reveal truth. It reveals truth by means of fiction, and that of course is what a parable is—truth hidden in fiction—truth in fiction.

Also published by
Greyladies

THE FAIR MISS FORTUNE
by D. E. Stevenson

Never before published, this charming story was originally written in the 1930s, when it was thought to be too old-fashioned to appeal to the modern market.

Jane Fortune causes a stir when she arrives in Dingleford to open a tearoom. Charles and Harold both fall for the newcomer, but her behaviour seems to vary wildly – first she encourages one then the other and at other times barely recognises them.

This edition also contains fascinating letters about the book between D. E. Stevenson and her agent.

EMILY DENNISTOUN
by D. E. Stevenson

Emily Dennistoun lives alone with her elderly tyrannical father at Borriston Hall on the Scottish coast. She has few friends and lives through her writing. Then she meets Francis, and despite vicissitudes of fortune, despite uncertainties, loneliness and unhappiness, Emily holds steadfast to a love she knows is true.

Originally entitled *Truth is the Strong Thing,* the themes of truth and honour pervade this rich multi-layered novel. Written at the beginning of her career in the 1920s, it has never before been published.

This edition includes an introduction by D. E. Stevenson's granddaughter, telling the story of the finding of the box of unpublished manuscripts by this much loved author.

PORTRAIT OF SASKIA
by D. E. Stevenson

Kenneth Leslie, needing money to start a new life in Canada after a broken engagement, answers an advertisement in the Daily Clarion –

Retired Army Officer offers a large sum of money to a Young Man who wants Adventure. Must be of good appearance and free from dependents

– and finds more than he dreamed of: fishing, art, family skullduggery, rogues, thieves and fisticuffs, friendship – and romance.

Also included are four short stories: *Moira, The Mulberry Coach, The Secret of the Black Loch, The Murder of Alma Atherton,* and a novella, *Where the Gentian Blooms.*

Previously unpublished, these are some of the manuscripts 'Found in the Attic' by the author's granddaughter. They were probably written in the 1920s, and foreshadow her later romances and family stories with that little humorous twist of something extra.

JEAN ERSKINE'S SECRET
by D. E. Stevenson

This is one of the early unpublished D. E. Stevenson manuscripts recently 'found in the attic' by the author's granddaughter. Probably written c.1917, it opens in 1913 with the Erskine family moving from Edinburgh to the Scottish east coast village of Crale, where Jean's life is transformed by her friendship with Diana MacDonald of Crale Castle. She writes a book telling Diana's story; of friendships and love affairs, of family and village life, all shadowed by the much darker themes of the Great War and devastating inherited conditions. And at the heart of the story is the secret, known only to Jean, that threatens Diana's hard-won happiness.